Jerry Snodgrass was born in Butler, Missouri, in 1938. He was raised and went to school in Indianola, Iowa. He entered the military after graduating from high school in 1957 and successfully fulfilled his dreams of serving in the military and federal service, traveling to worldwide exotic locations for over fifty years. Jerry is a Vietnam veteran and is a Life Member of the Veterans of Foreign Wars and American Legion.

His passion for mystery, suspense and the secrets of people who live in small towns inspired him to write *Shadows on Diablo Ridge*. He provides exciting reading with a fictitious mystery-suspense-romance novel set in current-day New Mexico. Jerry lives in Austin, Texas, with his wife, Rosemary, and their little Yorkie, Stormy.

To my wife, Rosemary. Thank you again for your support in writing this story. I love you. To my readers, I hope that you have at least half as much fun in the reading of this book as I've had in writing it.

To my good friend, Command Sergeant Major US Army (Ret), Jerry M. Stone. You are one of the main reasons I write my stories. I love you, brother.

Jerry Snodgrass

SHADOWS ON DIABLO RIDGE

AUSTIN MACAULEY PUBLISHERS™
LONDON · CAMBRIDGE · NEW YORK · SHARJAH

Copyright © Jerry Snodgrass (2019)

The right of Jerry Snodgrass to be identified as author of this work has been asserted by him in accordance with section 77 and 78 of the Copyright, Designs and Patents Act 1988.

All rights reserved. No part of this publication may be reproduced, stored in a retrieval system or transmitted in any form or by any means, electronic, mechanical, photocopying, recording or otherwise, without the prior permission of the publishers.

Any person who commits any unauthorised act in relation to this publication may be liable to criminal prosecution and civil claims for damages.

A CIP catalogue record for this title is available from the British Library.

ISBN 9781528946797 (Paperback)
ISBN 9781528971959 (ePub e-book)

www.austinmacauley.com

First Published (2019)
Austin Macauley Publishers Ltd
25 Canada Square
Canary Wharf
London
E14 5LQ

This is a work of fiction. Names, characters, business, events and incidents are the products of the author's imagination. Any resemblance to actual persons, living or dead or actual events is purely coincidental.

Other Published Novels by Jerry Snodgrass

While Justice Sleeps
Night Shadows over Sandy Creek
Man from the Sea
Woodcrest 911 (Kurt Chapel Series)
Crystal Lake Secrets (Kurt Chapel Series)
Castle on the Rhine
Forgotten Honor
Broken Triangle
Moments to Remember 1957
Memories – The Class of 1957
Lone Star Destiny
Frontier Justice

Book Description

On a September morning in 2018, a tall stranger steps off of the AMTRAK train in the New Mexico's sparsely populated southwestern town of Little Creek. His name is Dallas McCall from Big Spring, Texas. He is a former Marine and a combat veteran of the war in Afghanistan. The purpose of his visit is to find out who murdered his Marine friend, and a local rancher near Diablo Ridge. Dallas rents a Jeep from the pretty woman who owns and operates the local garage and gas station in Little Creek. Her name is Lori Porter who assists him with the investigation of finding who killed Dallas's good friend, Carlos Garcia. Carlos's sister, Carla, who runs the ranch for her father, becomes involved with Dallas, and the trouble he runs into with local rancher hired hands bullies. Dallas runs into a rich rancher and his son along with his friends who are prejudice against the Mexican ranchers, and attempt to make them sell their ranches. Dallas faces many obstacles, and his life is threatened as he closes in on the people who killed his friend Carlos on Diablo Ridge.

Chapter 1

September 19, 2018

The warm, late morning sun laid over the vast, yellow-brown emptiness of New Mexico's sparsely populated southwestern town of Little Creek. A tall, lean man, big-shouldered with coal-black hair stepped down from the AMTRAK train platform. He placed a brown canvas flight bag and a small leather bag down beside him and spoke quietly with the white-haired train conductor. The tall man smiled and pressed a twenty-dollar bill into the palm of the old man's weathered right hand.

"Thank you, sir, for ensuring my package is securely stored in the telegraph office."

The conductor smiled. "Good luck to you, young man."

Dallas McCall looked in the direction leading to the central part of town and spotted a hotel sign located halfway down the street on the left side. He slowly began walking with a slight limp carrying his bags toward the hotel. Along the way, he glanced at the old storefronts and sun-beaten rows of adobe-style houses scattered among the dusty streets.

As he continued along the sidewalk, Dallas felt the eyes of people that were walking and sitting on benches and chairs along the street following him. On his left, he noticed an elderly man with a white beard sitting on a bench, smoking a pipe outside of the M&J Bar & Grill. The man quickly got up and walked away down a nearby alley between the buildings. Dallas halted, looked around as the people continued to eye him suspiciously. No one spoke to him, and he had no reason to talk to them. *Yep, the small-town curiosity of a stranger in their town.*

As he neared the hotel, a group of three men, having a conversation together standing in front of a hardware store, ceased talking as Dallas approached them. They exchanged glances with each other and continued their discussion after Dallas walked past them.

When he arrived at the front entrance of the weather-beaten hotel, a large, barrel-chested man with squinty eyes, a scruffy beard and wearing a straw cowboy hat stepped in front of him blocking the doorway.

"Anything I can do for you?" the man said in a loud, gruff voice.

Dallas glared at the man, his eyes cold. "You run this hotel?"

"Nope."

"Then there's not a damn thing you can do for me except move the hell out of my way."

Dallas brushed by the man and entered the hotel and into the tiny, musty smelling lobby. A middle age, chubby, bald man wearing a white shirt and bow tie with black suspenders holding up his corduroy trousers came out of a room to the left and walked up to the front desk and dropped his eyes to an open register log book without looking at Dallas.

Dallas sat his bags on the floor. "I'd like a room."

"We're all filled up," the man replied immediately in a high-pitched voice, without an attempt to smile or make eye contact with Dallas.

Dallas glanced at the key rack behind the clerk, shifted his body weight and fixed calm piercing eyes on the man. "You have a lot of room keys hanging up there on the rack."

Without turning around to look at the keys, the clerk said with a hint of sarcasm in his voice, "They're for reserved guests." He still made no attempt to look at Dallas.

Dallas, quickly losing his patience said, his voice hard as stone, "Yeah, right. Any idea where I might find a room?"

"You might try the sheriff's office; he usually has an empty cell." The chubby man grinned and glanced at the large man Dallas had words with outside and a skinny, little man with a creepy smile on his face with a black cowboy hat pulled down on his ears standing near the front window.

Dallas heard the two laughing behind him. Without turning his head, he stared at the grinning clerk's red face. "Do you have a good dentist around here?" Dallas said, his voice filled with anger.

With a surprised look on his face, the clerk jerked his head up to look at Dallas for the first time. "Dentist, yes, of course, we do. Why do you have a toothache?" A smart-ass grin crossed his face.

Dallas's eyes narrowed. He said with anger in his voice, "No, no I don't, but you will need a dentist to replace your teeth if you continue giving me your wise ass remarks. Now, I am going to ask you one more time. Where might I find a room?"

The clerk stepped backward away from Dallas, a startled look on his face. He then mumbled, "There is a bed and breakfast located at the end of the street across from the drug store."

Instead of saying anything else to the clerk, Dallas glared at him for a few seconds, retrieved his bags, turned and stalked out of the hotel without acknowledging the big mouth who attempted to block his entrance to the hotel and the small, wiry man with a black cowboy hat standing in the lobby with smirks on their faces.

The two ranch hands from the Denton Ranch, John Badger and his little friend Weasel watched Dallas walk towards the Bed & Breakfast.

"I'm going to kick that stranger's ass," Badger roared.

"I'll help you," Weasel said laughing.

It was easy finding the Bed & Breakfast since it was the only house that stood on a corner across from the drug store with a sign in the front yard. *Little Creek Bed & Breakfast.* Dallas climbed the steps leading to a wide porch and a wood entry door with bevelled decorative glass.

Standing behind a reception desk was a tall, dark-haired middle age woman. "I'm Mrs Norris, the owner, welcome to my Bed & Breakfast." Her voice was cordial but not overly friendly when she told Dallas that she had a vacancy. He signed his name to the register at the front desk. The woman told him what the daily rate was and the hour's breakfast is served.

She handed him a key with the number 3 stamped on a green plastic tag with the name of the B&B printed in bright yellow letters. "Your room is at the head of the stairs on the right. I hope you will be comfortable Mr…Mr McCall," she said, glancing at the name on the register log.

Dallas nodded and smiled. He picked up his bags and walked toward the stairs that led him up to his room. The room smelled fresh, and with a quick look around, it appeared to be clean. There was a queen-size bed, nightstands on each side of the bed with table lamps. A dresser set in the corner with a recliner sitting near the window with a small-screen television located against the wall. He saw a small refrigerator and microwave sitting on top of the frig. The bathroom had a bathtub and a walk-in shower. *This will do just fine for me.*

He travelled light with only his needed essentials and a few changes of clothing in a light brown Marine Corps flight bag. At the bottom of his leather bag was a plastic ziplock bag with six medicine bottles that were filled with pain pills, and a white envelope addressed to him with a return address of Little Creek, New Mexico.

It was near noon when he left his room and went downstairs. Mrs Norris was standing behind the front desk. She smiled. "Is your room satisfactory?"

"Yes, it is very nice, thank you. Is there a place in town where I can rent a car?"

"Yes, there is a garage down the street across from the train station that sometimes rents vehicles. The only other location for car rentals is the next town east of here about thirty miles away."

"Thanks." He laid his room key on the desk, turned and walked out the door on to the porch and down the steps. He stopped, looked around and then began walking toward the train station, the area where the garage was located. His leg was hurting and throbbing from wounds he received from a Taliban fighter in Afghanistan six months ago. Reaching into the front pocket of his jeans, he removed a small bottle and shook two white pills in the palm of his hand and then threw them in his mouth and swallowed a couple of time to get the pills down. *Come on, pain-pills, do your job.*

He passed a grocery store, dollar store and several unoccupied buildings before arriving in front of the train station. Across the street, Dallas saw a white building with what looked like an office on one end and an open door with a lube rack on the other end. The faded white and green sign above the front door to the garage read: *Porter's Garage.* The single overhead garage door was open and faced the street. In the front of the building was parked a battered older model red GMC pickup truck, and an old WWII model Jeep painted olive drab with a light-brown canvas top.

He noticed the hood raised on a white pickup truck in the stall inside of the garage. As he approached, he smelled the distinct odour of oil and sawdust scattered on the cement floor. He saw a rather small backside of a person wearing baggy green coveralls with their body halfway inside the engine compartment.

Dallas stopped a short distance from the side of the pickup. He said casually, "Howdy…is the owner of the garage around?"

A female voice came from the person working under the hood. "I'm the owner; I'll be with you in a minute."

Before Dallas could speak again, standing in front of him stood a tall, beautiful woman with red hair protruding from under a green baseball cap with green eyes that seemed to glow in the dim light of the garage.

"How can I help you?" she asked in a soothing voice.

"Howdy, I'd like to rent a vehicle, a 4-wheel drive SUV or pickup, preferably a Jeep if you have one?"

Her eyes quickly examined Dallas from the tip of his cowboy boots to the top of his head. She smiled and placed a finger on the corner of her mouth. "I've never seen a man with blue eyes and black hair before – Are you part Cherokee Indian?"

Dallas chuckled. "I might have a little Indian blood in me. Do you have a vehicle that I can rent?"

Lori's eyes rested upon Dallas's eyes and for a moment, their eyes locked. "Yes, I just happen to have a Jeep available. How long do you want it for?"

"Oh, a couple of days or so should do."

"The charge is twenty-five dollars a day plus you pay for the gas. If that meets your approval, you can come with me to the office, and we can do a little bit of paperwork."

She removed the hat from her head and threw it on the shelf behind her; flowing red hair dropped down over her shoulders. "Are you able to drive a stick shift?" she asked bluntly.

"Of course, why do you ask?"

She grinned. "I saw you limp a little is why I asked."

Dallas snapped. "Just an old football injury that comes and goes."

"May I see your driver's license and a credit card, or cash if you prefer."

He removed his driver's license and Visa card from his billfold and threw them on the counter.

She picked up the license and credit card and looked at the driver's license. "Dallas McCall from Big Spring, Texas. What brings you to our friendly little town?"

He smiled at her statement about her town. "I'm looking around for the family of a close friend."

"Oh," she said, "maybe I can help you out, I've lived here almost all of my life. My name is Lori Porter."

"Nice to meet you, Miss, or is it, Mrs Porter?" *Now is not the time to inform people that I am looking for the family of my dead friend, Carlos Garcia.*

"It's Miss. Let me know if I can help you out with your search. We don't get many strangers around here as you can probably tell."

Dallas nodded. "Yep, an unwelcome stranger stirs up curiosity in a small-town that's for sure."

After he signed the rental contract, Lori smiled and handed him the ignition key hanging from a brown leather key strap. "No need for a map, there's nothing but dust and wasteland around here." A sheepish grin crossed her face.

"Thanks." Dallas left her standing at the counter, as he turned and walked away toward the parked Jeep without speaking another word or looking back at Lori standing at the desk with her mouth open.

Dallas walked around the Jeep and inspected it carefully for any damage. He then climbed into the driver's seat, started the engine, pulled the gearshift lever into first gear and sped off heading west into the vast, emptiness of the south-western New Mexico's mountains and open prairies. As he gained speed, the warm wind felt good to him as it whirled through the open sides of the Jeep.

After Dallas drove away from the garage John Badger, and his little loud-mouthed friend with the black cowboy hat, Weasel, arrived at the garage driving Badger's red Ford Bronco.

Lori was standing in the open garage door looking out toward the west wondering where Dallas was headed and what he was really doing driving around in the mountains and foothills. *This man may be looking for more than friends.*

John walked rapidly to where Lori was standing. "Who was the guy?"

She turned away from him and walked to the lube rake in the garage. "Just a man who wants to take a ride in the desert. Why do you want to know who he is?"

"Come on, Lori; give me his name and where he's from," John said in a demanding voice.

She replied, with disgust in her voice, "He is just a stranger in town. His name is McCall, and he comes from Texas. That's all I have to tell you."

John pounded a big fist on the garage doorframe. "That man could be here to interfere with our plans to buy out the Mexican ranchers and run them out of town. Don't you dare side with him if he asks questions? You can't turn against your friends." He glared at Lori and quickly turned and returned to his Ford Bronco with Weasel running behind him trying to catch up.

After the two had driven away and Lori was alone, she thought. *Friends my ass. You will never be my friend, John Badger. I wonder why they are so interested in Dallas McCall. He is a handsome son of a gun that's for sure. He may be a law enforcement agent, FBI or a serial killer, who knows. I need to find out more about that Texas man and what he is looking for. Badger may be right; he could be here to cause trouble between us, locals and the Mexican ranchers. Not my business, I have nothing against the Mexican population. Besides, most of them are my friends.*

Chapter 2

Dallas admired the rose-coloured desert landscapes on the right side of the winding road and the foothills and the mountains on the left side.

When he was five miles out of town, according to the Jeep's odometer, he spotted an old wooden marker, hanging at an angle at the side of the road, 'GARCIA RANCH'. Beneath it, an arrow pointed straight ahead. The mountains were to his left, not far away, and he caught sight of the road ahead of him. He steered the Jeep up to the entrance of the narrow, rutted road and weaved the Jeep between rocks and large boulders.

As he drove to the far end of the rock formation, he reached a flat stretch of land entirely surrounded by juniper-dotted hill's bathing in golden sunlight. Beyond the rocks, in the valley, stood a white adobe ranch house with two barns, and fenced corrals. "Now that is cattle country," he said out loud.

Yep, just as Carlos described it to me, 15,000 acres of prime high desert, grassland with a large stock pond for their water supply. He popped two pain pills in his mouth and washed them down with water from a plastic container. He then reached up and brushed a tear from his eye, thinking about his friend and how much he missed the happy laughter of Carlos.

He drove down the lane toward the house and parked near the walkway leading to a long, wide covered porch.

He was met by two barking dogs that looked vicious to him. A young Mexican boy ran out of the front door toward the Jeep. He called the dogs to his side and waited for Dallas to turn off the engine of the Jeep.

Dallas climbed out of the driver's seat and stretched his stiff leg. When he took a few steps towards the boy and the dogs that had stopped barking and were sitting beside the young boy, his dark eyes staring at him. He was slim in build, and black hair fell on his forehead.

"You must be Christian?" Dallas said with a friendly smile.

The boy turned his head as if he did not hear Dallas speaking. Then a friendly grin spread across his face, and he rushed toward Dallas.

"You are my brother's Marine friend from Texas?"

Dallas held out his hand. "Yes, I'm Dallas McCall, and I'm happy to meet you. Carlos shared his family pictures with me. I've seen many photos of you, and I feel as if I've known you for a long time. How old are you?"

"Thirteen, sir." The boy pumped Dallas's hand, and tears rolled down his face. "Please, come inside and meet my mother and father. They both have been sick lately, and it's hard for them to get around like they usually do."

When Christian opened the front door to the house and Dallas walked into the open living room, a small older woman with silvery hair sitting in a wooden rocking chair began to cry. "Oh, my lord, it's Carlos's friend. We are so happy you came to see us." She held out her arms toward Dallas and motioned for him to come to her.

Rosa Garcia, the mother of Dallas's good friend, Carlos placed her hands on the sides of Dallas's face. "Our Carlos loved you and wrote us about you in all of his letters." She turned in her chair to face the frail man sitting next to her. "Romon, this is Carlos's Marine friend, Dallas McCall from Texas."

The man smiled and held out his hand to Dallas. "Welcome to our home, son. We are so happy our Carlos had such a good friend to look over him while he was fighting the war in Afghanistan. He looked forward to you coming here to visit him and to meet us after he came home from the Marines. How nice of you to come and visit us and pay respect to Carlos' gravesite. Please stay with us. Our daughter, Carla, is out tending to our cattle. She will prepare an excellent meal for us when she returns."

Dallas being a former combat Marine held back his tears, but the sadness inside him would not go away thinking of his friend.

"Thank you, I would like that." *I didn't do so well to protect him. I was in Texas when he was murdered by bullets from an unknown assassin near his parent's ranch. I should have been here with him when he asked me to visit and help him with a problem he encountered and a threat to his life and that of his family.*

The sound of the door opening from the back of the kitchen interrupted Dallas's thoughts.

Stepping into the room came a strikingly beautiful young woman with a brown cowboy hat on her head with black hair flowing down her back. She was wearing a blue shirt, jeans that clung to her shapely body with brown leather chaps cowboy boots with Mexican Charro Spurs.

Her brother met her, saying with excitement in his voice, "This is Carlos's Marine friend from Texas, Dallas McCall."

She did not smile and only glanced toward Dallas. "Nice to meet you." She smiled at her parents and walked into the kitchen without saying another word.

Dallas was shocked by her cold reception towards him. *Carlos had always told Dallas his pretty sister sure liked to look at our pictures together and commented on what a handsome friend he had from Texas.*

Christian broke the cold silence. "You must forgive my sister as she is so bitter and sad about Carlos being killed and no one has been arrested for his murder."

Dallas dropped his head. "I understand. She may blame me for not coming to visit Carlos after we both were discharged from the Marines. I was working with my father on our ranch and could not get away to pay a visit to him."

"She will get over it," the father said. "We are grateful for your friendship, and to finally meet you in person is wonderful. How about we drink some wine?"

Dallas smiled. "Sounds good to me."

Romon poured the wine, and Carla was in the kitchen with her mother. By the aromas of Mexican spices and the smell of olive oil coming out from the kitchen, they were preparing a traditional Mexican meal.

Dallas could not stop thinking about how Carla reacted to meeting him. *I know she blames me for not being with Carlos's before he was murdered.*

The young brother, Christian, sat quietly listening to his father and Dallas talk about the ranch and how much Carlos loved the life of a cowboy. "He was an excellent rider and roper," Romon said, his eyes full of tears.

Dallas noticed an 8 X 10 photo of Carlos wearing his dress blues, sitting on the mantle of the fireplace. Next to it was a smaller picture of the 14-man elite Marine Raider Team that Dallas was the team leader of and Carlos was the assistant operation's sergeant. He remembered clearly. *Three of those brave men are dead. One of them, Carlos.*

Carla and her mother prepared the most delicious Mexican meal, Dallas; a native Texan, had never eaten. There were corn tamales with tomatillo salsa, green chile beef enchiladas, tacos, charro beans, and fudgy chocolate Mexican brownies for dessert.

Carla was quiet while they ate, and Dallas caught her making eye contact with him a couple of times, then she quickly turned her head away when Dallas moved his head to meet her glance.

After dinner, as the adults sat at the table drinking coffee, Dallas announced, "My visit to you is special to me. Besides paying my respects to you and honour Carlos, I have something to share with you." He removed an envelope from the back pocket of his jeans and laid it on the table in front of him. "Carlos wrote me this letter just before he lost his life last month. I thought it may help law enforcement with their investigation as to who is responsible for Carlos' death."

Carla picked up the letter and read it out loud speaking in English:

"20 July 2018
Hey, Amigo,

How are you doing down there in Texas? I bet your momma is putting some meat on your bones with all of her home cooking. I'm doing pretty good and enjoy working on the ranch to help out my dad and sister. My parents are not doing well, but they are up in age and have worked hard all of their lives with little to show for it but their ranch.

My sister and little brother are having a hard time when they go to town and when my brother is in church summer school. There are a group of real assholes that work on nearby ranches that hang around town. Needless to say, they have an intense hatred towards us Mexicans. Last week, I got in a big fight with two of the cowboys and beat the crap out of them. Their ranch manager, the owner's son, Ty Denton and two no accounts threatened to kill me and burn down my folk's ranch.

You know what I told them. Come near my family, and I will put a bullet square between your eyes. That didn't go over so good. I shouldn't have threatened them.

Come on over to see me, and we can take a trip down to Mexico. I will take you up into the mountains and my favourite spot, Diablo Ridge. You know I do speak Mex!

Take care, my friend, write me if you remember how. Semper fi, brother.

Your Amigo,
Carlos"

Carla tossed the letter on the table and kicked her chair back and stormed into the kitchen and out of the back door, avoiding Dallas's eyes as she moved past him.

Dallas sat without speaking, thinking to himself that he probably made a mistake and should not have shared the letter with the family.

"It will be alright," Romon said, placing his hand on Dallas's arm. "You were right by sharing Carlos' letter. We know about the troublemakers and how they hate us and want us out of the valley. There are no other Mexican families except the Morales and Mendoza's that will stand up to them along with us. They are too powerful and have large, prosperous ranches. Somehow, we will find someone to help us find out who murdered our son."

Dallas drew a slow breath and glanced at the family as his eyes met theirs. "That is why I am here. I am the person who will do my best to bring Carlos's killers to justice. I have the know-how to hunt down predators without them knowing they are being hunted. Our main concern is to keep your family safe and away from outsiders harassing you. Are you in agreement for me to work undercover and find the people who took Carlos's life?"

Romon's eyes welled up with tears, and his wife sobbed quietly. Christian wiped a tear from the corners of his eyes with his shirtsleeve.

Romon replied, "Of course, you have our support. We will help you any way we can. Our house is your house for as long as you need."

"Thank you, I appreciate your generosity. Now, I had better get back to town as not to alarm the curious people of Little Creek." He gave Romon his cell phone number before leaving. "Call me anytime you need me. I have a room at the Little Creek Bed and Breakfast owned by Mrs Norris."

As Dallas drove off heading back to town, he saw Carla standing firmly in the middle of the dirt road in front of him, her hands on her hips. He slammed on the brakes, and the Jeep stopped within inches of her.

"Damn, woman. I could have run over you," he said as Carla moved to the driver's side of the Jeep.

She looked directly into Dallas's surprised face. "Sorry I was so harsh and ugly to you. I know it was not your fault that Carlos was killed. I just wanted you to know that." She gently slapped him on the arm and handed him a small folded piece of paper, and then she turned and quickly walked back toward the house.

He unfolded the paper. It was her cell phone number with a note. *Call me if you need help.*

Looking off toward the Garcia ranch and the Jeep driving away through a pair of high-powered glasses is John Badger. He said to his friend, Weasel, sitting in the passenger seat of his Bronco.

"So, McCall is friends with the Mexicans. We will find out what he is doing coming to our town and associating with the Garcia's. Mr Denton will want to know that the stranger made a visit to the Garcia ranch."

Weasel laughed. "We need to kick his ass and run him out of town."

Badger merely grunted, "We will do just that, and soon."

Chapter 3

During breakfast at the B&B on Friday morning, Dallas was the only person in the dining room. Mrs Norris filled his cup with coffee, and for the first time, an amiable smile crossed her face.

"Am I the only guest you have today?" Dallas asked.

"Yes, right now you are. I get feed salesman and cattle buyers in during the first part of the week. Are you sure your room is satisfactory?"

"Yes, ma'am. It is very nice, thank you."

Seeing the happy smile on her face as she walked towards the kitchen made Dallas smile. *I bet she is a widow. She's a lovely looking woman.*

After breakfast, Dallas drove to Porter's Garage to request a rental extension on the Jeep. As he pulled into the garage parking area, he saw a red Ford Bronco speed away back toward the middle of town.

Dallas spied Lori standing under the lube lift, observing a man draining the oil out of the crankcase of a car sitting on the rack.

She saw Dallas and walked out of the garage to meet him as he climbed out of the Jeep.

"Your Jeep runs good; it serves my purpose. I would like to extend my rental contract for another few days."

"It's no longer for rent," she said sarcastically without looking at him.

Dallas, with a surprised look on his face, replied, "It was for rent yesterday. What's the problem?"

Lori, her head lowered staring down at her boots, snarled, "I have other plans for the Jeep."

"Someone must have told you something about me that changed your mind. Yesterday, you agreed to rent me the Jeep for a couple of days." Dallas glared at Lori, but she would not return his eye contact. "What in the hell is wrong with this unfriendly damn town of yours anyway?"

She jerked her head up and glared at Dallas. "There is not a thing wrong with this town. What concern is it of yours anyway?" Her voice was filled with anger.

"Everyone seems to be concerned with me and treating me like I am an enemy from outer space or an IRS tax collector."

"Sorry. Things do change. You want to give me the key?" She held her hand out.

Dallas handed her the key. "Do you have some sort of a problem with me scouting around in the foothills and open prairies?"

She jerked her head up and looked up the street toward town. "Whatever you're up to, Mr McCall, I don't care. I own and operate a business and have to go on living here. These people are my neighbours, my friends."

Dallas shook his head in disgust. "I respect your wishes, Miss Porter. You have a nice day and enjoy your friends." He turned and commenced walking up the street toward the town, thinking about how he could get to the nearby town to find another vehicle to rent.

It was near noon, so Dallas decided to stop by the M&J restaurant and grab a bite to eat. He sat upon a stool at the counter and ordered a bowl of chili and iced tea from an unfriendly swarthy-looking man wearing a white apron that took his order. The smell of stale grease filled his nostrils, and he heard the sizzling of hamburger meat on the grill behind the open counter.

The door to the restaurant flew open, John Badger, the little man, called Weasel and a nice-looking young man dressed in western attire entered and took seats at a table a few feet behind where Dallas sat.

The booming voice of John Badger carried through the room. "Hey, you, stranger. You still around? I thought you didn't like our little friendly town."

Dallas was already pissed off by the woman at the garage not renting him the Jeep. He turned on the stool and looked toward Badger. "If you're talkin' to me…yep, I'm still around if it's any of your goddam business." He swung back around and stared at the bowl of the chunky brown looking mixture the café called chili sitting in front of him on the counter.

Dallas heard snickers coming from the three men. Then he heard Badger's harsh voice again. "I think you've got my stool!" He laughed. "Did you hear what I said, Mexican lover?"

Not wanting any trouble, thinking the local sheriff was probably good friends with the men, Dallas laid a five-dollar bill on the counter, swung the stool around, rose up to his full six feet three inches and walked toward the door.

As Dallas passed the table Badger, grabbed hold of Dallas's arm and spun him around. Now, the two men were facing each other, their faces filled with anger.

Dallas shook free of Badger's grasp and ducked the man's sucker punch to his midsection. With a series of lightning fast jabs from Dallas's fists, the would-be fighter lay unconscious, face down in the middle of the table among broken water glasses and condiments. Blood trickled from his nose and the corner of his mouth.

Dallas stood back from the table and fixed his eyes on Weasel and then the on to the young cowboy. They two both held their hand's palms up towards Dallas and pulled their chairs away from the table.

"We don't want any trouble, mister," the young cowboy yelled out.

With a hard glare in his eyes, Dallas took a step toward the cowboy and spoke in a firm voice. "I don't know who you are, and I don't give a damn. My name is Dallas McCall, and I was friends with Carlos Garcia. And for the record, I aim to find out who murdered him. So, if any of you are involved, be aware. I will track you down and make you wish that you were never born."

None of the men moved or spoke, their eyes focused on the stranger who just beat the crap out of the town's toughest man.

Dallas turned quickly and walked out of the restaurant. His injured leg hurt after the fight. He took two pain pills and ambled back up the street toward his room.

As he approached the B&B, he saw the Jeep that he had rented yesterday parked in the guest parking area. *What in the hell is the pretty redheaded woman from the garage doing here?*

Upon entering the lobby, the owner, Mrs Norris was standing behind the reception desk. "I have an envelope for you, Mister McCall," she chirped.

Dallas took the white envelope. "Thank you." He opened it on the walk up the stairs to his room. Inside the envelope were the key to the Jeep and a handwritten note. *Mr McCall, rent the Jeep for as long as needed. When you have time, please stop by the garage. Respectfully, Lori Porter.*

He went into his room and laid the key and note on the dresser. *I wonder what changed the woman's mind about me. I need to find out if her reason is business or is she trying to find out more about me and what I'm doing in Little Creek riding through the mountains and prairies in her Jeep.*

The next change of events happened when Dallas left his room an hour later. As he walked down the stairs, he saw a middle-aged man wearing a white cowboy hat and a tan uniform. As he neared the man, he saw the gold sheriff's badge pinned on the shirt above the left breast pocket.

"Mister McCall, I'd like a word with you."

"Sure, what can I do for you?" Dallas answered.

"I'm Dan Baker, sheriff of Canyon County. Let's talk outside on the porch."

They walked out onto the wide porch. The sheriff pointed to wicker chairs sitting to their left.

After they were seated, the sheriff said, "I hear you had a run-in with John Badger today."

"I don't know a John Badger, but I did have a few words with a loud mouth man who took a swing at me at the M&J restaurant around lunchtime."

The sheriff grinned. "Well, that was John Badger, and he has filed a complaint against you for assault and battery."

Dallas leaned back in the chair, grinned and casually said, "We call it self-defence where I come from. I was only defending myself from being attacked."

"Well, you sure as hell did that. You broke his nose and knocked out two of his teeth, and his jaw is fractured. Where is it you come from, Mr McCall?"

"Texas, Big Spring, Texas."

The sheriff finished writing in his notepad. "Are you a registered martial arts expert?"

"No, not me."

The sheriff trained his eyes on Dallas. "I take it you are a military man?"

"Was. United States Marine Corps."

"Are you a combat Marine?"

Dallas nodded his head. "I am. Three combat tours in Afghanistan."

"Well, that answers most of my questions. I am a former Marine myself; first Gulf War. If you are planning to stay in town, I want to know more about what you are doing here in Little Creek. Stop by my office before you leave town."

"Will do. Semper fi." Dallas smiled, and so did Sheriff Dan Baker as he walked away down the sidewalk.

He said, 'stop by my office before I left town.' Why did he think I was leaving town? The sheriff must be the prime investigator in Carlos' murder. I need to speak to him and find out if he is an honest cop or on the take from someone. I sure could use his help, and he could use my assistance.

That evening, a disturbing rumour crept through the town of Little Creek. It seems as though the stranger in our town is a secret agent or a private detective looking for whoever murdered Carlos Garcia. The word from witnesses is – "He threatened to hunt down and kill the killer."

The diners in the restaurant could not stop talking about the stranger who whipped John Badger. One man said to the three men he was talking with. "It was like out of a movie or TV fight scene. That tall man was so fast with his fists, knocking old Badger to the floor in less than five or ten seconds. He must be a CIA agent or some drug cartel guy."

Chapter 4

Nine o'clock Saturday morning, Dallas stopped the Jeep in front of Lori Porter's open door to the garage.

She looked over her shoulder from where she stood in the shadows of the back wall of the garage cleaning tools when she saw Dallas climb out of the driver's seat and walk toward her.

Lori kept her back to Dallas as he stopped a short distance behind her. "Miss Porter. I appreciate you changing your mind about extending the rental agreement on the Jeep."

Without turning around, she said, "Business is business, and lord knows, I need the business. I heard that you beat the crap out of old John Badger. He is an asshole and the bully of the county. I'm sure he deserved what you gave him."

"I can't stand loudmouths and bullies. He should stay clear of me for a while. There was a younger man with him and that little Weasel guy. The younger one fit the image of a cowboy. Any idea who he is?"

Lori turned around to face Dallas. She stared at him for a few seconds. "Yes, it must have been Ty Denton. His daddy owns a big ranch west of here about ten miles. He is a spoiled college brat that does what he wants and takes whatever he wants. He's trouble, so stay away from him."

"I have another question for you. Did you know Carlos Garcia?"

Lori seemed to jump when she heard Carlos's name. "Why, yes, I knew him well. He was a nice young man and so respectful to everyone. It's a shame that he was killed. Did you know him?"

"Yes, I knew him well. We were in the Marines together, and he was a terrific and loyal friend. When the name Garcia comes up, people around here seem to get hostile. Do you know why that is?"

"As I told you before. I don't want to get involved with other people's business. The majority of the Anglo folks around here are prejudice against the Mexican ranchers. It has caused many hard feeling between the American and Mexican ranchers. Most all of the Mexican people I know around here are Mexican-American, and their ranches have been in their families for generations. Nearly half of the town population of 1,500 is Hispanic, and the families have occupied the town for years. The Garcia family are all good people. I liked Carlos, and I know his sister, Carla. She is a nice person and a good rancher with a sound business mind."

"Well, thanks for the information. Have no worries with me keeping my mouth shut. I don't want to hurt your business. I keep what is told to me to myself. I hope that you have the same values."

"I sure do. Now, if you will excuse me, I have work to do. Oh, you get a five cent a gallon discount when you gas up at my gas pumps." She giggled as she walked away.

Dallas drove steadily over the rough, rocky terrain toward Diablo Ridge leading to the Garcia ranch coming in from the north side of the ranch, away from the main curvy road leading from Little Creek.

He drove along the narrow winding road with high cliffs rising on one side and falling off steeply on the other. The compressed sandstone walls smoothed, rounded and etched by centuries of the constant winds coming from across the mountains.

The Jeep jerked, and the front end came off of the rocks but continued to move steadily to the top of the high ridge.

When Dallas reached the crest of the ridge, he spotted the Garcia ranch house and buildings in the rose-coloured valley below. He stopped the Jeep and climbed out and walked along the edge of the rim. He saw the reflection coming from the water in the stock pond to the south of the ranch house, and cattle grazing on the pastures were mere specks.

The ranch is set in a perfect location. Romon's forefathers indeed choose the right spot to build their ranch. I am wondering if Carlos' death had anything to do with investors wanting to buy the land.

It was still late morning; the sun had just cleared the mountains, as Dallas approached the driver's side of the Jeep when bullets suddenly peppered the rocks behind him, the sounds of the gunfire echoing through the ridge. He flattened himself on the rocky surface, and the rounds kept coming, sending rock splinters over his head and around the side of the jeep. *Holy shit, this is like Afghanistan all over again. By the sound coming from up there and the rapid-fire, the shooter must be using a semiautomatic rifle, like an AR-15 or carbine. Why in the hell would anyone want to ambush me? And me hiding here without a weapon...damn!*

Suddenly, the gunfire ceased, and all was quiet. All Dallas heard was the sound of the swirling wind coming over the Rocky Ridge. He raised up just enough to see over the hood of the Jeep, looking in the direction where he thought the gunfire came from. Dallas held his position, listening for any sounds that would alert him whoever was shooting at him were moving in to take more shots at him. After a short time, he heard the sound of an engine in the distance. He thought whoever was doing the shooting had fled away in a small truck or on an ATV, or a four-wheeler of some sort.

I need to get the hell out of here. Keeping low, he climbed into the driver's seat, cranked up the engine and drove down the steep ridge road toward the sun-filled valley in front of him.

He drove the rest of the way to the Garcia ranch without incident. When he parked the Jeep in front of the ranch house, the sun was directly above him. Christian and his dogs met Dallas as he climbed out of the driver's seat.

"Hello, sir. You are just in time for lunch," the boy said with excitement in his voice.

"Lucky me. It seems as though I arrive just about when it's around meal time."

Carla came out of the kitchen door wearing skin-tight jeans and boots, a broad smile across her face as she approached Dallas and her brother.

"Hello, Dallas. It's nice to see you again. Come on in, we're about ready to eat lunch."

"Thanks, sounds good to me. Oh, nice to see you again also."

During lunch, consisting of a Mexican beef casserole, Dallas told the family about him being ambushed up on Diablo Ridge.

"I have no idea why anyone would be taking pot shots at me. I've only been in town for a few days, and already I have enemies who want me out of town – or dead!"

"If you don't know, Diablo Ridge is where Carlos was killed?" Romon said, wiping a tear from his eye. "You are lucky that you were not injured or even killed. Who are these people and why are my family and you being targeted?"

"No, I didn't know that is where he died. I remember him talking about how the ridge was his favourite location to be alone and do his thinking. I plan to visit the sheriff and ask to see a copy of the investigation of Carlos' death. I think the key to Carlos' death, the threats against your family and the attack on me comes from people living in and around Little Creek that know we are friends."

Carla said, "That is what Dad and I think. Sheriff Baker seems to be an honest man, but his hands are tied by the lack of deputies and the political power the owner of the Denton Ranch and his hired thugs who run the town."

"Yes, I ran into a couple of them on my second day in town. Are you up to telling me about what happened leading up to when Carlos was murdered?"

Carla said, "Yes. Carlos always had a ledger, even before he enlisted in the Marines. He kept a daily log of what he was doing. He told us that it was necessary to maintain a current daily log when he was in the Marines. I'm guessing that you must do the same? The problem is, we cannot locate the ledger. Carlos must have made entries that he did not want us to see."

"Yes, I do keep one. Hopefully, you will locate it. Knowing Carlos, I'm sure he went into detail with his entries."

Carla wiped a tear from her eye. "Christian helps me every day searching for the ledger, but we are running out of places to look."

Romon, who sat by quietly chimed in, "The day he died, we all were waiting for his return to the ranch and repeatedly called his cell phone when he did not return for dinner. At eight o'clock, we saddled horses and headed out toward the ridge to search for him. Several hours later, we found him dead on the ridge, leaning against his ATV with multiple gunshot wounds to his body and head."

Romon dropped his head and cried quietly.

Dallas reached over and placed his hand on Romon's arm. "I promise you that I will find out who took Carlos away from us. If the sheriff doesn't find the killer, I will find him, I swear on Carlos' grave."

"God bless you, my friend," Romon said with sadness in his voice.

Dallas managed a smile. "I'll be back and visit you soon."

On the slow drive back to Little Creek, Dallas could not get out of his mind the way Carlos died. *He was targeted that's for sure, but why would someone want him dead? I know for a fact that he was not a troublemaker. He stepped on someone's toes, and it's up to me to find the answers.*

That evening, before the M&J café closed, Dallas stopped by and ordered a plate of red chili enchiladas and a bottle of local beer for his dinner. An older Hispanic woman with a half-smile working as the waitress took his order. A vast difference from the unfriendly man who was working during the daytime the first time he was here. There were only a few people were dining, and Dallas enjoyed the peace and quiet of having a meal without hearing the boisterous voice of John Badger and his little friend blasting through the dining room.

After he finished eating, Dallas decided to take a drive around the town, hoping to find out more as to why the local people were so unfriendly towards him. *I know that a stranger coming to a small town will always be a stranger. It appears to me that the townspeople are afraid or hiding a secret, just as Lori mentioned to me.*

As he drove past building after building sitting empty and worn in time among the constant wind, hurling dust, and open prairies surrounding the little town of Little Creek, he saw three churches, one Methodist, one Baptist, and one, a Catholic church. *It's like a town frozen in time.*

It was two-thirty in the morning when Dallas awoke from a troubled dream. He went to the bathroom and splashed cold water on his face, then sat down in the chair next to a window, staring out at the scattered lights along the empty main street.

There are many secrets in this little town. Someone out there is a killer, and there are people in town that know who that person is. It is the job of the sheriff to conduct the investigation. I've got to do more to find out who murdered Carlos, and why.

Chapter 5

The next morning, a little before nine o'clock, Dallas left the Jeep parked and set out walking from the B&B down the street to pay a visit to the office of County Sheriff Dan Baker just two blocks away.

He felt the usual suspicious eyes of the town folks upon him as he crossed the street and walked stiffly up to the entrance of the sheriff's office. Out of the corner of his eye, he saw a man sitting on a chair at the end of the building. The man removed his feet from the top of a litter can that set in front of him and quickly turned his head away from Dallas when he looked his way.

He must be the town spy! Dallas smiled.

Dallas decided it was best not to mention the attack on him at Diablo Ridge to the sheriff during his visit. He entered the office. It is small with sunlight coming into the room from full windows facing the street. There were two desks, with straight chairs sitting beside each desk. The usual police posters hung on a bulletin board on the wall. He saw an open door to the side of the room that led to the dark and stale smelling cellblock.

Sheriff Dan Baker appeared from another door behind one of the desks. "Mister McCall, glad you stopped by. Have a seat." He pointed to the chair beside the desk with a wooden nameplate, '*Sheriff Dan Baker*' sitting at the front centre of the desk.

Dallas sat down. "You asked me to stop by before I left town. Here I am, and I'm not ready to leave your town just yet."

The sheriff suppressed a grin. "Appreciate you stopping by. I have a few more questions to ask you that I never got to on our first visit." The sheriff lowered his eyes peering at the inside of a folder lying on his desk. He raised his head and bluntly asked, "Mr McCall. What exactly are you doing here?"

Dallas stared harshly at the Sheriff. "I will answer your question with a question of my own."

"Fair enough. Fire away." The sheriff leaned back in his chair and observed Dallas who sat rigid in the chair next to his desk.

"I am here to visit the family of a Marine friend of mine that was murdered on Diablo Ridge on August 5. This location is in your county. My question to you is. What are you doing to find out who killed Carlos Garcia?"

The sheriff seemed surprised by the abrupt reply of Dallas and quickly sat straight up in his chair. "We have little to go on except the body of Carlos, and his ATV that his body was propped up against when his body was discovered by his family. The autopsy report revealed he died from multiple gunshot wounds to the torso, leg and a close-up shot to his head by a .308 calibre bullet shot from a Winchester hunting rifle. The size of the wounds to his legs was from a smaller calibre and could not be identified. The killer must have been staring Carlos in the eyes when firing the fatal shot to his head."

Dallas asked, "Have you spoken to any of the local men I've seen hanging around town who could have held a grudge against Carlos? Being such a small town, most everyone should have known who Carlos was, being a local rancher and decorated Marine."

"No," the sheriff exclaimed. "I have not. I have no authority to ask every man in town if they killed Carlos Garcia. Yes, I think most all of the people around town knew who he was."

With disgust in his voice, Dallas said, "I have a letter written to me from Carlos a few days before he was found murdered. He specifically named a ranch owner's son, Ty Denton and two other men that they threatened to kill him and burn his parent's ranch down. He also said threats were made against his sister and young brother by local men in town who have a dislike towards Mexicans."

"Do you have a copy of the letter?"

"Of course I do," Dallas snapped.

The sheriff responded to the harsh tone of Dallas's voice by replying in a loud voice. "With your permission, I would like to make a copy of the letter to add to the investigation file."

Dallas reached into a back pocket of his jeans and pulled out a white envelope. He handed it to the sheriff. "I hope I can trust you?"

The sheriff suppressed a grin. "Of course you can trust me! I am probably one of a few in this town you can trust."

The sheriff got up and walked to the copy machine sitting by a window. After he made a copy of the document, he returned the letter to Dallas.

"For the record, sheriff; I'm going to investigate Carlos' murder on my own. I aim to find out who killed my friend with or without your help."

"I can't stop you from what you plan to do. Just don't cross the line of the law and keep me informed of what you uncover. For all I know, you may be an undercover FBI agent or a private investigator. Either way, finding the people who killed your friend is a top priority for my department and me."

"I appreciate your time," Dallas said as he pushed back the chair and stood up. "The FBI did not send me here, and I am not on hire to conduct the investigation. You know where to find me, unless Mrs Norris, owner of the B&B, kicks my ass out."

The sheriff asked, "Who sent you here?"

Dallas's eyes wavered briefly, and then he grinned. "I just told you. The truth I know it was – my conscience!"

"Have you killed men other than in combat?" the sheriff bluntly asked.

Dallas's face became a mask. He did not answer the question immediately and glared at the sheriff. "No, I have not."

The sheriff then leaned back in his chair and looked at Dallas. "Remember, Mister McCall, don't take the law into your own hands."

"Affirmative." He turned and walked out of the office.

The sheriff seems like an honest lawman, and I like him. I intend to continue searching for the people who killed Carlos. Since people are shooting at me, it's time to pay a visit to the telegraph office and pick up my package stored there. He must think that I am a dangerous man. He got that right if I find out who killed Carlos before he does.

Chapter 6

One block down from the sheriff's office, Dallas saw the sign; *Postal Telegraph Office* arched across the front of an old brick building.

Upon entering the office, Dallas saw a middle-aged man with reading glasses perched on the end of his nose sitting in an old straight-backed chair with a newspaper held up to his face. The man lowered the paper and jumped up when he saw the stranger standing rigidly at the counter.

"What can I do for you, sir?" the man said in a weak, squeaky voice.

"I have a package stored here. I want to pick it up. McCall is the name."

"Yes, sir, Mr McCall. I'll be right back." He walked to the back room and returned within a few minutes, carrying a package about the size of a shoebox. The man sat it on the counter in front of Dallas.

"Is there a charge?" Dallas asked.

"No charge. The conductor of the AMTRAK train took care of the fee."

"Thanks," Dallas turned and walked out of the office. During the slow walk back to the B&B, he gave more thought about him being ambushed on Diablo Ridge, and why or who did the shooting. *There sure as hell is a hidden danger on that ridge. Carlos, talk to me, buddy.* He grinned at his thoughts about Carlos talking to him.

After returning to his room, Dallas removed the heavy brown wrapping paper from around the box and removed the top. Inside was a Glock 19M 9mm service pistol and four 15-round magazines and a black hip pancake holster. He removed the handgun, inserted a magazine and pulled back the slide and released it, loading a round in the chamber. *Now, you back shooting cowards. I'm ready for you.*

Dallas drove to Lori's garage and was putting gas in the Jeep when she appeared from the open garage door. He watched her walk towards him, her body swaying with the stride of a graceful animal.

"Is the Jeep running okay for you?" she asked in her cheerful voice.

"Yes, no problems so far. Well, all except the muffler bearings make a lot of noise." A smirk crossed his face.

She laughed. "Yeah right, you're talking to a real mechanic here. Where are you headed to today?"

Dallas returned the nozzle to the pump and screwed on the Jeep's gas cap and looked at Lori, who was giving him the eye. "Oh, just taking a ride out into the wide-open spaces."

"That sounds like fun. Believe it or not, I've not taken the time to enjoy the leisure of riding in the prairies and foothills for a long time."

Dallas saw the excitement in her eyes. "Why don't you take the day off and join me. I promise not to take advantage of you." A mischievous grin curled up at the corners of his mouth.

She laughed. "I might just do that if you're sure you won't mind my company."

"How could I mind a beautiful woman riding around in her Jeep with a stranger she barely knows?"

"Give me five minutes." She rushed back inside the open garage door and spoke to the man standing at the rear of the garage.

When she returned, her greasy green coveralls were gone, replaced by tight jeans and a white T-shirt that held nothing back from showing off her well-formed breasts. Her red hair fell over her shoulders; her face glowed with excitement. She jumped into the passenger seat and smiled at Dallas. "Let's go, cowboy."

He smiled at her and drove off towards the road heading west. As they sped down the long empty two-lane curvy road, Lori turned in the bucket seat, looking back toward the town in the distance. "I have always dreamed that someday I would be leaving Little Creek forever." She slowly turned back around and trained her eyes on the road ahead.

Out of the corner of his eyes, Dallas glanced at her lovely features and her red hair flowing back in the wind like a tail on a running horse. *I wonder what her story is? She is too damn pretty to not be married. I can tell she is highly educated. I don't have much time to find out, but maybe she will tell me more about herself as the day goes by.*

Lori turned her head toward Dallas and blurted out. "How old are you?"

There was almost a smile on his bronzed face. "Twenty-eight. How old are you?"

She calmly answered, squinting her eyes, "Twenty-six; I turned twenty-six in July."

As his eyes sweep the road and countryside, he did not catch the admiring glance she was giving him.

"Have you ever been to Diablo Ridge?" Dallas asked.

"Yes, once, or maybe two times a long time ago."

"Do you remember much about the area?"

"Yes, I think so. Why?"

"If you don't know…that is where Carlos was murdered. I felt his spirit when I went there a few days ago."

Lori replied, "Yes, the whole town knows Carlos was discovered dead up there on the ridge by his family. I feel so sorry for them; and for you, being a close friend with him."

Dallas sat quietly his eyes trained on the narrow road in front of him. He pulled a small amber-coloured bottle from his shirt pocket. He opened the lid and emptied two white pills into his left hand and popped them into his mouth, and washed them down from the water bottle sitting in the middle console.

Lori looked at him quickly. "What are the pills for?"

"Distemper." He glanced at her and grinned.

"Yeah, right. I saw you limping. Have you been injured?"

He nodded his head. "Yes, a few times."

"So, I guess you don't want to talk about it."

Dallas replied without turning toward Lori, "No, there is no reason to burden you with my life story."

She shifted her body, so she was facing Dallas. "Who are you after?"

He answered her question almost immediately, "Whoever killed Carlos."

"You're looking for trouble – you know that, don't you?"

"I've faced trouble before." He felt her eyes glaring wildly at him.

She gently placed a hand on his arm. "You can trust me. I can help you if you want me to."

As he drove, he quickly glanced at her, and then looked back toward the road. He then said, "How can you help me without your friends turning against you?"

She gave a half-laugh at the blunt question. "My real friends will remain true to me. They know what has been going on around the county and in Little Creek for years. Some good God-fearing men and women keep quiet to protect their families. The bad people are the ones that keep the hate going between the Anglos and Mexican families."

Dallas slowed the Jeep down and said, "The Denton Ranch is out this way, right?"

"Yes, we have been driving along their property for the past fifteen or twenty minutes. There is a turn-off just ahead of us where we can get a good view of the main house and ranch facilities."

Dallas pulled the Jeep to a halt, and they got out and walked to the edge of a bluff that overlooked the high prairie grasslands below. They could see the sprawling ranch house standing in the glaring sun, surrounded by a green lawn, surrounded by a white fence. There were trees spread around the house, and they could see a long porch extending to the edge of the house. Beyond the house toward a high bluff stood a cluster of sheds painted white. They made out an extra-large barn and three corrals.

"That's a hell of a big ranch down there. They must own thousands of acres," Dallas said.

"Yes, I heard that they own over 200,000 acres of prime ranch land. The old man, Bill Denton very seldom comes to town. His son, Ty, runs the ranch along with long-time hired hands. He is the one you asked me about. The little cowboy named Weasel is a hired hand and he, along with John Badger, another hired hand, is always with Ty where ever he goes."

"From what I can tell from up here, the Garcia ranch connects to the Denton Ranch from the northeast. How well do you know Ty Denton?"

"Not very well. Ty was two years behind me in school, and I never liked him, and I don't like him now. He is a spoiled asshole that always looked down his nose at us blue-collar people, and especially the Hispanic population. Him, Weasel, and their buddy, John Badger are always bullying people. I bet old Badger will never screw with you again after the ass whipping you gave him."

Dallas grinned. "Do you know of any conflicts between Carlos and Ty Denton?"

"Oh, yeah. The two fought on quite a few occasions over the years as they were growing up. Carlos beat the living shit out of Ty after he came home from the Marines in July. Witness's heard Ty threaten to kill Carlos after Carlos drove away in his pickup."

"Any idea what the fight was about?"

"I heard that Ty told Carlos that he and his father would force Carlos's father to sell his ranch to them. Carlos flew off the handle and left Ty lying bleeding in the dirt in front of the hotel. Later that afternoon, the sheriff brought Carlos into his office for questioning. He was released a short time later with no charges against him."

Dallas frowned. "I need to have a talk with Ty Denton." His eyes drifted off towards the far side of the brilliant sun-filled valley below.

Lori moved a couple of steps closer to where Dallas stood. "You do know that if you confront Ty, you will have to deal with Weasel and probably John Badger."

He grinned. "That's true. I'm not too worried about those two."

Lori looked at the tall man with admiration and smiled. "They don't scare you, do they, cowboy?"

"No, not at all. We should head back to town. You are probably losing business by being out here with me."

"I don't think so. Besides, I kinda' like being with you."

A smile touched the corners' of Dallas's mouth. "I kinda' like being with you my own self."

During the drive back to town, they were silent exchanging glances and smiles with each other. Lori talked occasionally, pointing at an area of interest along the road as they drove by them.

Lori broke the silence, "A penny for your thoughts, cowboy."

He glanced at her and smiled mischievously. "You would probably slap my face if I told you."

The truth was Dallas's deep thoughts about what his next move would be. *Something positive will turn up – I hope!*

After dropping Lori off at her garage, Dallas stopped by the local grocery store to stalk up on a few snacks, lunch meat, cheese, bread, potato chips, bite-size Butter Fingers, and a six-pack of beer to store in the refrigerator in his room.

He was amused at the stares and whispering coming from the few shoppers who were mostly women. The middle-aged woman at the checkout counter only made eye contact with Dallas once, and that was when she gave him back his change from the twenty-dollar bill for the groceries.

"You're welcome," Dallas said, startling the rude checker. He gave a quick look over his shoulder at the two women standing behind him in the checkout line. *Better close your mouths, or you will catch flies.* He laughed to himself at his macho sense of humour.

He returned to the Jeep in the parking lot, and his thoughts returned to earlier in the week when someone used him for target practice on Diablo Ridge. *I'm going to find out who took those pot shots at me. Someone sure wants to drive me out of town! That someone is probably the person I am looking for that may have murdered Carlos.*

Later that afternoon, a dark dust cloud coming in from the western prairies swirled rapidly along the main street as Dallas entered the Little Creek Tavern. A few men were standing at the bar, others sitting on high stools. There was the usual array of bottles and glasses aligned before a cracked, discoloured mirror. In the corner, there stood a 1950s era jukebox with Carl Perkins singing, Blue Suede Shoes coming out of the speakers.

Dallas made his way to the bar in the rear of the room. He stood, his elbows spread out, leaving little space on each side of him, preventing someone wanting to occupy his space.

"What will it be?" The burly man behind the bar asked.

"Local Beer...Draft." Dallas, sombre-faced, turned his head slightly and scanned the open room. To his left sitting at a table near the front window, he recognised John Badger, Weasel, and the young cowboy, Ty Denton.

Dallas took a gulp of the cold beer, licked the frost from his mouth and grabbed a handful of peanuts from the dish sitting in front of him on the bar. Behind him, he heard the cackling laugh of Weasel followed by the disgusting laughter of Badger.

Suddenly, a burst of anger came over Dallas. Without warning, he picked up the mug of beer from the bar sitting in front of him, turned quickly and threw the glass mug into the middle of the table of the laughing local loudmouths.

Badger fell back in his chair, sputtering, and wiping the beer and broken glass from his face. The room went silent, except for Carl Perkins voice coming from the jukebox. Ty, Weasel nor a man in the room moved or spoke a word.

Dallas, his eyes and face filled with anger moved to the table and faced the three surprised men. "That is a warning, and it will be your last one. If anyone of you tries to scare me into leaving town, or if I hear as much as a simple threat against me, I will make your life a living hell. Another thing, if you make another attempt to shoot me in the back, beware! I will hunt you down like a wild animal. Denton, we need to talk!" A hard glare continued from Dallas's eyes. With a sharp turn of his body, he was gone out of the front door.

He was still fuming when he entered his room. *I'm not sure if I did the right thing or not. At least, I got their attention. McCall, you need to watch your temper.*

Back in his room, Dallas sat in the recliner near the window and closed his eyes, attempting to take a short nap. The demons and ghosts in his mind did not permit him to do so. His eyes were closed, but the hallucinations of war took over his mind.

After eating supper in his room, consisting of a bologna and cheese sandwich and a beer, Dallas received a call on his cell phone from Carla Garcia inviting him to their ranch on Saturday for a BBQ with the family and friends. She asked him if he would like to stay the night with them. "Christian has an extra bed in his room, and it would make him so happy to be with you."

Dallas readily accepted. *It will be nice to sleep in a house filled with family instead of a lonely room at a bed and breakfast.*

It was a little past ten o'clock when Dallas took a short walk around the quiet, empty streets of town, hoping the exercise would help him sleep. The air was cool and fresh coming in from the mountains and open prairies. *Nighttime in Little Creek is the only peaceful part of the day. I bet this could really be a charming town after the people responsible for killing Carlos is found and brought to justice. I sure as hell will not be counted in their census.*

As he lay in bed, Dallas's mind again drifted back to Afghanistan six months ago and how fortunate he was to still be alive. *The sun was sinking low down in the rugged western foothills of Afghanistan. I was close to dying. There was one chance in fifty that I might live two or three days, but there was no chance at all that I would live more than three. I knew that a team of Marine Raiders was searching for me after I got separated from my group.*

The bullet which a Taliban fighter had sent into my leg two days before had left a large wound, and the blood ran freely into the last of the combat gauze from my medical pouch, draining life from my body.

The thought that I was dying did not chill me, or make me afraid, or cause me to cry for mercy. The last thing I remembered was listening to the tramping of fast-moving feet racing toward where I laid surrounded by blood flowing from the gaping wound in my leg.

Two weeks later, sitting up against two hard pillows in a hospital bed at Landstuhl Regional Medical Center, Germany. I did not look like a man who came close to death fifteen days ago. I remember outside of the hospital room window, it was spring, the glorious spring of the German countryside. It reminded me of my home in Texas. I remember my thoughts that day, and I will never forget the feeling in my heart. I'm alive, and I damn well will do everything in my power to stay that way.

He woke up, his underwear and T-shirt soaked in sweat. After he washed his face in cold water and put on clean sleeping clothes, he went back to bed, praying for a horror-free sleep. His prayers were answered as he drifted off to a quiet sleep for the first time in months.

Chapter 7

The Denton Ranch
10:00 O'clock That Evening

John Badger, Weasel, and Ty sat on a u-shaped couch in the family room, facing Bill Denton, Ty's father who sat in a brown leather recliner sipping on Kentucky Bourbon from a personalised square glass.

There was a tightness around Bill's mouth when he said, "I can't believe that you three grown men would let a stranger make asses out of you. What the hell is he even doing in our town? Do any of you know why?"

"No, not for sure, Dad," Ty replied. "He has been asking questions about the Garcia's and the death of Carlos Garcia, but we don't know why. He might be some sort of CIA agent or a hired assassin. He is a tough son of a bitch that's for sure."

Bill replied, "I can sure as hell agree with that." He gave Badger and Weasel a dirty look and then stifled a grin. "He may be a private detective looking into the murder of Carlos Garcia. The last I heard, the sheriff does not have a suspect or clues as to who murdered him. I told the sheriff he should bring in the Feds to look into the murder. Carlos was a good kid, and I like his family. It would make the Garcia family very rich if they accepted my offer to buy their ranch."

Ty, Badger, and Weasel exchanged quick glances. Ty spoke in a weak voice. "Dad, can you call your police friend in Albuquerque and see if he has anything on this McCall guy? He doesn't have any business being here poking his nose around town and asking questions. He is dangerous."

Bill laughed. "Maybe we need more strangers coming to town, so we have more to talk about than the price of beef. If it makes you boys feel better, I'll give Police Chief John Collins a call tomorrow morning." He fixed his eyes on the three sitting in front to him. "You boy's sure you don't know anything about the death of the Garcia boy?"

Heads were nodded without answering Bill's question.

Bill said, "Ty, I have a meeting tomorrow with two company representatives from Albuquerque. They are billionaire investors, and they mentioned to me yesterday that they wanted me to go in with them in buying out the Garcia ranch along with the other Mexican cattle ranches. It's an attractive long-term investment opportunity for us. I want you to be with me."

Ty grinned. "That would be perfect for us if we could own more land. We already own a mega ranch – with 100,000 more acres added to our 200,000 acres that would make us multi-millionaires."

Bill's laugh was short and harsh. "Us, you said us. You have not earned the right to tell me you own my ranch. When you grow up and show me you are mature enough to run the ranch on your own without me and the hired ranch workers looking out for you and keeping you out of trouble then I may name you a co-owner."

Ty was embarrassed that his father ran him down in front of his friends. He shrugged his shoulders without looking at Badger or Weasel.

"Now, you boys get on out of here so I can have a little peace and quiet," Bill said in a gruff voice.

The following afternoon, Police Chief John Collins returned the call to Bill Denton with a report on Dallas McCall.

"He has no criminal record," the Chief told Bill. "He resigned his commission from the Marines as a Captain after eight years of service in July of this year. He is a highly decorated and Purple Heart Recipient combat veteran, and his home of record is Big Spring, Texas."

Bill Denton thought. *This man could be trouble. I hope to hell Ty doesn't do anything stupid to piss off the stranger more than he already is. I sure don't want to lose my son over real estate investing.*

It was one o'clock when Bill and Ty met the white and blue helicopter as it landed in the pasture near the ranch house. Two men, wearing business suits and carrying black bags ducked their heads as they emerged under the helicopter's spinning blade toward Bill and Ty sitting in an ATV nearby under a clump of shade trees.

"I'm Bill Denton, this is my son, Ty. Welcome to the Denton ranch." The four men quickly shook hands.

"Please, get in, and we go up to the house," Bill said.

Ty took off walking ahead of the men and was waiting on the covered patio for his dad and the two men when they arrived. Bill told Ty to make sure their kitchen help had the table prepared for the guests.

"Have a seat, gentleman. My cook has prepared a light lunch for us. If you need to use the bathroom, Ty will show you where they're at."

The men sat down in the cushioned patio chairs. The taller of the two men smiled and said, "I am Lester Taylor, this is John Waters. As you are aware, we represent the P.J. Conner Corporation, and we have our sights set on buying and investing in ranch land. It is our understanding that two companies from Fort Worth have been in contact with you. We hope to persuade you to work with us and not have a battle with other bidders."

Bill smiled. "That is what we want also. The last thing I want is a showdown and a battle to buy cattle ranches. Our problem is that the ranchers, all Mexican owned, do not want to sell their properties. Their ranches all have Waterland, and the price of cattle is up."

John Waters laughed. "Money talks and we have the money to pay them on the spot cash for their land. The Connor Corporation wants the area around here to develop into large cattle operations, wildlife ranches and resorts. This will be a prosperous long-term investment for you, Mr Denton. With your assistance in, say...strong-arming the Mexican ranchers to sell, will bring you enormous wealth."

Ty's eyes flashed, and he grinned at his father.

Bill replied, "I don't mind a little tough talking, but as far as threatening anyone, that is not what I do. I don't dislike the Mexicans; I just want their land. Hell, they would all be rich if they sold to us."

Lester Taylor spoke up in a commanding voice, "Mr Denton. If you plan on dealing with our corporation, then you must use an approach that will work to persuade the ranchers to sell their ranches to us. The markets for the properties in this area are high and larger companies are preparing to join in buying up the ranches."

"What is it you want me to do?" Bill asked.

Lester spoke again, "Talk with the Mexican ranchers and encourage them to sell their properties to us. Hell, tell them anything. Time is running out for us before we get into a showdown with our competitors. I suggest you hire men to assist with convincing the owners that it is time to sell and move out of the valley to a quiet life in the city."

Bill said, "Cattle ranching has been about the only way to earn a living in these grasslands since the late 1800s. The people are not going to turn tail and run."

"Maybe you are not the right person we are looking for," John Waters said, his voice harsh.

Bill turned quickly and moved nearer the man. "Mr Waters, I was born and raised on this ranch, and I have never had any problems whatsoever with my neighbours, Anglo or Mexican, and I don't aim to start a land war just to get rich. If you don't want to deal with me, then get your ass back on your whirlybird, and I will make a call to Fort Worth to my other business contacts."

Lester broke in, "Take it easy, Mr Denton. I don't think John meant what he said to you. We want to deal with you, and we will back you with your methods of dealing with the ranchers. Please keep in mind that we are working with a large market, and time is essential. I will contact you with an update on our corporation's marketing plan. In the meantime, we would like for you to reconsider your nice guy approach and give thought to be a little more forceful."

Bill did not reply to Lester's remarks. He extended his right hand toward Lester, shook it and then squeezed John's hand.

The corporation executives walked to the waiting helicopter. The pilot started the rotors and lifted the little helicopter up and flew north.

Ty said, "Damn, Dad. I've never seen you like that before."

"There are a lot of things you don't know about me, son. One is my respect for honest, hardworking men and women." He left Ty standing, thinking about what he told him as he disappeared into the house.

Maybe I have not tried to understand my father. He is a tough man that's for sure. I know he doesn't like my friends, John Badger and Weasel. I could try to help dad out without him knowing I'm doing it. He is the good-guy – I can be the bad guy. I aim to own this ranch one day and run it the way I have always wanted to do without being bossed around and treated like a little boy by my father.

Chapter 8

Saturday afternoon beneath brilliant blue New Mexico skies, guests began arriving at the Garcia ranch for the day's festivity.

"We are so happy you accepted our invitation for a fun-filled weekend of a traditional family Mexican fiesta and BBQ," Carla said to Dallas as they mixed with the smiling happy faces of the Garcia family and their close friends.

"Oh, I like your gray lizard boots; they go well with your blue shirt and jeans," Carla said smiling.

"Thanks. You fill out your jeans pretty good yourself."

The day was sunny, with a cool breeze blowing in across the valley from the mountains which made it possible to have the tables filled with a variety of food arranged around the front on the house under the shade of old Sycamore trees.

Romon, his wife, Rosa, and Christian found Dallas and Carla talking with guests all holding bottles of Corona beer in their hands.

"I see that you are in good hands," Roman said, placing his arm around his daughter. "If you will excuse us, we must welcome the new guests who are arriving."

Dallas gazed with interest at the couple walking into the yard where they were met by Romon and Rosa. Dallas could not help but notice a man, a nice-looking Mexican gentleman who was big and tall with thick silver hair and a matching silver beard. The woman with him was tall, slender, with long black hair streaked with silver, and she had a bright, beautiful smile on her face. Dallas thought she was a very elegant looking lady.

"Who is that couple talking with your parents?" Dallas asked Carla.

She raised her head looking toward the foursome. "Oh, that is my mother and father's long-time friends, Miguel and Ivanna Mendoza. They own the ranch to the west of us. They are wonderful people. I don't see their son, Diego, with them. He doesn't come out to many functions. Come with me, I will introduce you to them." She hooked her arm through Dallas's arm and guided him around the guests who were talking and laughing in small groups.

Dallas was introduced to the Mendoza's. Romon said to Miguel and Ivanna, "Dallas and our Carlos were best friends when they were in the Marines fighting the war in Afghanistan. We are so happy that he came to visit us."

Miguel spoke in English with an educated voice, "We are so saddened by the death of Carlos. The investigation is being dragged out by the county sheriff, Dan Baker. My family put up a 10,000-dollar reward for the capture and conviction for those who were responsible for his death. You have our deepest sympathy for the loss of your friend."

"Thank you, sir. Carlos will forever live in my heart." Dallas felt moisture at the corners of his eyes.

Carla piped up, "Well, we'd better get over to the dinner tables, or these hungry people will eat up all of the food; especially the teenagers; they are always hungry."

"See you all later." She took hold of Dallas's hand, and he smiled as she pulled him away.

"That is a nice young man," Avanna said. "I do believe Carla has taken a liking to the stranger."

Romon and Rosa nodded and smiled at each other.

Christian finally caught up with Dallas and his sister as they sat at a long table filled with food eating and talking with the guests.

"Hey, you two," Christian said as he sat his little butt down between Dallas and Carla. He looked at Dallas. "I was wondering if you would meet my friends after you finish eating?"

Dallas smiled. "Sure, I'd be happy to."

"Good," he jumped up and patted Dallas on the shoulder and ran off.

"He really likes you," Carla said. "He misses Carlos so much, and I think he wants to adopt you as his big brother."

"I could never take the place of Carlos, and I will never try. I like your little brother, and I can see a lot of Carlos in him."

"He favored Carlos when he was thirteen. Christian is a good boy, and I hate to see him so sad. You make him happy!"

"He makes me happy also. You and your parents have done an excellent job of bringing him up the right way."

Later, Carla and Dallas found Christian and his friends all sitting on the edge of the porch drinking what Carla guessed was iced tea. The boys, around eight or ten of them welcomed Dallas with simple well-mannered courtesy greetings.

To Dallas, they all looked alike, tall and awkward, with brown faces and cowboy hats perched on their heads. *They sure are young Mexican cowboys.*

"We're all going to join the Marines when we finish school," said one of the boys. "Carlos told us we needed to grow hair on our butts before the Marines would let us enlist. Is that true?"

Dallas chuckled. "If Carlos told you that then it's true. You are spot on when you say enlist after you finish school. The Marines won't take you unless you finish high school."

"See you later," Christian said as he took off running with his friends.

When all of the guests had bid their goodbyes and left for their homes, Romon led Dallas to the front porch, where they were soon joined by Christian, Carla, and her mother.

"It's nice and cool," said Romon. "I want you to see the sunset over the mountains. Carlos never missed a sunset when he was growing up and when he came home on leave from the Marines."

"I like seeing the sun go down myself. At my parent's ranch in Texas, the sun hides under old oak trees standing around a small lake." He started to speak, but the words would not come out, "We...Carlos and I saw many of sunsets where we were at. The conversation always included watching the end of a beautiful day with our families." He dropped his head and tried to hide the tears rolling down his cheeks, thinking about how much he missed his friend.

Carla slipped her hand in his and gently squeezed his fingers. She then moved her arms and hips to meet the side of Dallas's body. Their eyes met and locked.

"Who's up for ice cream," Christian shouted, breaking off the eye contact between Dallas and Carla.

Carla nudged Dallas with her shoulder, looking up at him smiling. "Sounds good," Carla answered. "First, I want to show Dallas our picnic area down by the pond."

Romon and Rosa exchanged glances and smiled at each other.

"I hope you don't think that I am too forward by asking you to take a walk with me? I knew you were uncomfortable talking about Carlos."

"I'm pleased with your crafty idea. Besides, it's been a long time since I took a walk with a beautiful woman."

"No, I can't believe that," she said, laughing softly. "Don't you have a lady friend back in Texas?"

"No, not really. I was engaged to my high school sweetheart until she decided that she did not want to be married to a Marine who was at war all of the time."

"What happened between you two?"

Dallas grinned. "She married the son of a big car dealership man in Abilene while I was deployed to Afghanistan."

Carla giggled. "Sorry, it was her loss."

Dallas nodded and smiled. "That's what I thought."

Carla pointed in front of her. "There is our family recreation spot."

There was a covered picnic area with a fire pit with tree stumps for seats sitting around the pit, and a double-sized picnic table near a group of willow trees. They stood on the edge of the pond and looked out over the still water with the reflection of the late afternoon sun casting flashes of light across the water and through the trees lined up around the pond.

Carla said, "The pond is spring fed, and we always have water. This makes our ranch so valuable to the many people who want to buy us out."

Dallas thought, *Maybe the pond has something to do with Carlos' murder.* "This sure is a beautiful ranch. Having a constant water supply is so important to cattle ranching. You have a lot of responsibility doing most of the ranch work by yourself."

She nodded. "Yes, but Christian is coming along just fine. He is growing and will soon be strong enough to pull more of the load around here. Daddy's strength is improving every day. Since you've been around, we have seen his spirit rise. He misses Carlos so, and we think you hold a part of him inside your heart."

"I do. Now, miss newspaper reporter, tell me a little about yourself. Where are all the young men who should be hanging around you?"

She laughed. "I'm not into men who act like little boys as most of them do around here. Don't have time to fight them off me and listen to their bullshit stories about their talents. I've never had time for a boyfriend, and to tell you the truth, I'm not looking for any man to try and tame me and tell me what to do – no sir. When I do find the right person to love, he will be a man's man and not a boy." She glanced at Dallas and then looked quickly away.

Dallas could not help but grin. "Damn, you are a woman with strong feelings that's for sure. You have a rarity that most real women would like to have, and most men are scared of."

She looked up at him. "Do I scare you, Mr McCall?"

"Not much, but I do respect the hell out of you."

She smiled, looked down at her boots and moved her right toe around on the grass. "We better get back to the house before Christian eats all of the ice cream."

Dallas thought Christian would never stop asking him questions as they laid in their beds in Christian's bedroom located at the west end of the house.

The last time Dallas clicked on the light to the face of his watch, it was 1:25 in the morning. His thoughts were on the beauty of Carla and how much he enjoyed being with her. He finally drifted off to sleep with a smile on his face. The demons and ghosts in his mind did not visit him during the night.

Chapter 9

It was the next morning at seven-thirty when Dallas walked into the kitchen, raising his head to the smell of freshly brewed coffee and bacon being fried. The two blends was a favorite breakfast smell of Dallas.

Carla and her mom were standing at the stove. They both turned around and smiled. "Good morning, are you hungry?" Carla asked.

"I'm always hungry."

"Grab a chair there on the end of the table. I'll get your coffee. Do you like breakfast tacos?"

"Thanks, you bet I do."

When Carla poured his coffee, their eyes met and locked as they did the previous afternoon at the pond.

"Thank you," Dallas said, not taking his eyes off of Carla.

"Did Christian keep you up all night talking?" Carla asked.

"No, he was worn out and went to sleep immediately. I got the best night sleep that I've had in a long time."

She slowly turned away from the table and moved gracefully back to the stove. Dallas watched every step she took. *She sure fills out those jeans. Her butt is firm by sitting in a saddle. I like this cowgirl, but she is too young for me and out of my league. I need to stop flirting with her and encouraging her to flirt back with me. I'm giving her the wrong impression. She is a looker, that's for damn sure.*

Romon and Christian joined Dallas at the table, and they ate and talked about the party yesterday and how happy it was to be with all of their friends.

It was nearly eight-thirty when breakfast was finished. Romon and Dallas relocated to the front porch and sat in wooden rockers to admire the crisp morning air, listening to the call of mourning doves coming from the trees scattered around the pond. They sat quietly without speaking, drinking coffee and enjoying the solitude and companionship.

Romon broke the silence and turned his head and body to face Dallas. "Do you think whoever killed Carlos will ever be found?"

Dallas did not answer right away as he did not want to give Romon false hopes. "Yes, I do. I believe the sheriff is doing all that he can with the limited manpower that he has. Myself, I have a few ideas in my mind, but I'm looking for more clues before I can really put a plan together and come up with who is the guilty person or persons."

Romon replied, "Thank you for coming to help us. We trust you, and we will assist you in any way we can. I can see why Carlos respected you so much. You are a good man and a loyal friend."

"Thank you. Carlos would help my family if it were me that died instead of him."

Dallas sat quietly for a few minutes and then asked Romon, "Would you ever sell your ranch to outsiders?"

"No," Romon answered quickly. "I would never sell our ranch, not to anyone for any price. Bill Denton would pay top dollar for this property anytime I ever decided to sell. He knows that my ranch is not for sale, and it never will be as long as the Garcia family is alive."

Dallas nodded and smiled. "I thought so." *As long as the Garcia family is alive. Damn, could someone want all of the family dead so they can buy the ranch? Lord, I hope not!*

Romon then looked up at the morning sun and floating white clouds. A slight smile formed on his mouth. He breathed in deep and said softly, "Carlos is up there looking down on us; I can feel his spirit."

Dallas reached over and laid his hand on the shoulder of Romon. "Me too. I can feel his spirit, and he is guiding us to the cowards who killed him."

After lunch consisting of yesterday's leftovers and iced tea, Dallas bid his goodbyes and thank-you's to the Garcia family for their hospitality over the weekend. He said to the Romon, Rosa, Carla and Christian. "I liked all of your neighbours. It was an honour to spend time with y'all, and the food was excellent."

Carla made Dallas promise to call her. "Please be safe as there is danger lurking out there, as you are finding out, strangers in town are not welcomed by everyone."

"I heard that. I'll be careful. Appreciate your concerns with my safety."

Carla studied Dallas for a second or two. "You're special to us."

During the drive back to town, Dallas thought about his next move to gain more information about what led up to Carlos being murdered. *I know some townspeople know what happened to Carlos and who the killer or killers are. So far, Lori is the only person who has given me any meaningful information. On top of my list are John Badger, Weasel, and maybe Ty Denton and his father. I'll stop by the sheriff's office tomorrow and find out if he has come up with any definite clues.*

When Dallas picked up his room key from the front-desk, Mrs Norris handed him a sealed white envelope. "A young boy dropped this off for you this morning."

"Thanks." He smiled at her and walked up the stairs to his room. He sat down on the edge of the bed and opened the envelope. He read: *I have information for you about your friend, Carlos. Please come after dark. 203 Platte St.*

This could be a trap, or the person or persons may really have information for me. He glanced at his watch. 3:25. *I'll take a little nap before it gets dark.*

His attempt to catch up on his rest did not work out. Just when he would drift off to sleep, the nightmares that haunted him woke him up.

After one hour of tossing and turning, Dallas took a hot shower and soaked his throbbing leg. He swallowed two pain pills, dressed and ate a half of a cold meat sandwich and drank a beer.

He thought more about the mysterious person who wanted to talk to him about Carlos. "How does this person know that I am trying to find out who killed Carlos? The mysteries of a small town," he said, thinking out loud.

Chapter 10

It was seven o'clock when Dallas pulled the Jeep to a halt in front of a small one-story house, the exterior painted gray. He adjusted the holster that carried his 9mm pistol and walked up on the porch and knocked on the screen door.

While he waited, he turned and could see the lights at the hotel at the intersection lights and the streetlights of the main street running to the train station and Lori's garage. The door opened slowly, and a little gray-haired Mexican woman peeped out.

"Mr McCall?" she said in broken English.

"Yes, ma'am. I'm Dallas McCall."

She unlocked the screen door and opened it halfway, looked at Dallas and then fully opened the door. "Won't you please come in," she said, her voice uneasy and trembling.

Dallas followed her to an open kitchen with a square wooden table and four matching chairs sitting in the middle of the room under a hanging pink light fixture. He caught the delightful smell of Mexican spices.

The little lady placed her hands on the table, and with tired eyes, she looked at Dallas. "Young man, my name is Francisca Alvarez, and I am 86 years old. I live here alone as my husband died six years ago and my two daughters live in Santa Fe. I have known the Garcia family all of my life. Carlos went to school with my two daughters. I am so sad and angry about the death of Carlos. He was a good boy."

"Yes, he was a good friend of mine. We were in the Marines together. You mentioned in your note to me that you had information for me about Carlos."

"Pardon my manners. Can I offer you something to drink or to eat?"

"No, thank you, ma'am. I'm good."

"You must please promise me that you will tell no one that we talked and what we talked about. Can I trust you?"

"Yes, ma'am. You can trust me. I aim to find out the truth about Carlos's death, and I do not have much to go on."

She leaned in toward Dallas, as if she didn't want to be heard. "I sit on my porch every day when the weather permits, and I have a clear view down the street and the front of the hotel. I have a pair of binoculars that I use to watch the birds and the clouds over the prairies and mountains. I'm a snoop, I guess." She laughed softly.

Dallas smiled. "I think that is good for you to observe life around your home. Did you see something suspicious involving Carlos?"

He eyes widened before she spoke. "Yes, I did. I was sitting on the front porch looking through my binoculars, and it was near noon on the last day of July when a red station wagon or one of them SUVs pull up in front of the hotel. I saw tied to the top of the vehicle a woman. I made her out to be a young looking Mexican woman wearing a yellow dress. Four men got out of the vehicle; the driver was John Badger, and then I saw that man they call Weasel, and then I saw a man get out of the rear seat. I had never seen him before. He was dark, and I took him to be a Mexican. Then the Denton boy came out of the hotel, and he began shaking hands with the other three, and they were laughing and pointing at the woman tied to the vehicle. I could see her trying to move her hands. Then I saw Carlos standing motionless in the centre of the street behind the vehicle. Carlos moved up to the vehicle and cut the woman loose and helped her get down. He said something to her and then I saw her running down the street toward the west…" She leaned back in her chair and let out a deep breath of air.

"You need to rest a few minutes, ma'am. No need to rush into your story."

She shook her head, took a sip of water. "I'm ready to finish now."

"Whenever you want," Dallas replied.

She started to speak, but no words came out. After taking another swallow of water, she said in a weak voice, "I saw Carlos as he walked around to where the four men were standing with their backs to the vehicle and where Carlos stood. They were not aware that Carlos had freed the woman. Carlos ran up and grabbed John Badger by the back of his shirt and threw him to the pavement. The other three men turned away, quickly staring at Carlos, who was standing in a fighting stance. The man whom I did not recognise stepped toward Carlos, and Carlos knocked him to the ground. Carlos was shaking his fist at John Badger, the Denton boy and…what's his name, Weasel. Carlos finally turned and walked across the street and got into his truck and drove away. That's about all I recollect."

"That is a nice report, ma'am, thank you. I think that you already know that I am looking for whoever murdered Carlos which is why you contacted me. What you have just told me sheds a lot of light on what I'm looking for. The sheriff does not have this information, and as I promised you, he never will hear it from me."

Francesca placed her weathered hand on Dallas's hand. "Some people in town know the things that go on just as I do, but they're too afraid to talk."

"Who are they afraid of?"

"I think, mainly John Badger. He is a mean bully. The Denton boy, Ty, is protected by his father and some of the big Anglo ranchers. I have never heard of Ty hurting anyone, but he sure throws the Denton name around Little Creek and the county."

Dallas's grin was warm. "Thank you again, ma'am, for confiding in me. Your information is beneficial and important to me. If you don't mind, I would like to stop by sometime and sit with you on your porch and…snoop!"

Her smile glowed. "I would like that. I will fix you some good Mexican food, and maybe we will drink a beer."

"Thanks, I will take you up on that offer."

He was still smiling when he cranked up the Jeep and drove back to the B&B.

Back in his room, he was hungry. After downing a beef brisket sandwich and a piece of pecan pie that Rosa gave him when he left their ranch, he watched a little of the nine o'clock news on television, and then he went to bed and again fought the demons in his dreams.

The next morning after a breakfast of ham, eggs, hash browns, toast and cup after cup of coffee, Dallas made a visit to Sheriff Dan Baker at his office.

"Make yourself comfortable. I see you're still in town." The sheriff did not change his curious facial expression.

"Yeah, why shouldn't I be? Seems to me that there are a lot of people who would like to see me disappear. Are you one of them?"

The sheriff laughed. "Nope, not me. I was just pulling your chain. What have you been up too?"

Dallas brought the sheriff up to speed on what he had been doing about the murder of Carlos, leaving his personal life a secret. "I wouldn't want your job. These locals are tightlipped…or just plain scared of someone."

"The job of being sheriff is challenging. It appears that no one knows anything about what happened to your friend except what they have heard from gossip around town. You know how gossip escalates into false stories."

Dallas nodded. "Do you know or have you heard about any large corporations wanting to buy out the Mexican ranchers in the county?"

"Oh, yeah. There is talk that a land developer from Texas wants to buy up the land and build hunting clubs and dude ranches. The big ranchers are too powerful and are financially able to decline the high stakes offers. However, the smaller ranches, mainly owned by Mexican-American families are barely making ends meet. Their families have been landowners longer than most of the Anglo ranch owners."

Dallas shifted in his chair. "Do you think there may be a connection with the land developer and Carlos's murder? Money has no conscious."

Dan replied, "I've received no complaints from any of the ranchers about high-pressure tactics from outside corporations. It is possible that is a motive, but again, I have no evidence or proof about such actions."

"Well, thanks for your time, sheriff. I have nothing to add to our conversation. You know I will be out there looking for anything that will help me find out who killed Carlos. It was murder; there must have been some motive to kill him. There was no robbery, nothing is missing; the whole damn affair is a mystery."

"Stop by anytime. The coffee pot is always on," Dan said.

Dallas smiled and left the office and climbed into the Jeep parked in a reserved parking space marked, *Official Vehicles Only*.

As Dallas drove slowly down the main street toward Lori's garage, he looked to the west and could see the ridges surrounding Diablo Ridge. *Come on, Carlos, give me a clue, brother.* He managed a slight smile.

Dallas was putting gas in the Jeep when Lori appeared from inside the garage. "Howdy, stranger. What have you been up to? I haven't seen you around lately."

He smiled. "Not much, just hanging out and spending time with the Garcia family." *Damn, you look good. I would still like to know her story and why she is not with a man. I hope she's not gay!* He laughed to himself.

"How is the family coping since Carlos' death? I haven't seen any of them around since the tragedy in August."

"They are getting along with the support of each other. We never get over death."

"Tell me about it," she mumbled.

Dallas thought he understood what she said. He changed the subject. "Is there any problems with extending the rental agreement on the Jeep? I will need it a little while longer."

"Nope. No problems." She peeped around from the gas pump and looked at the meter. "Twenty-three dollars and fourteen cents. You want me to add that to your bill?"

"Yes, that will work. Speaking of work. Do you ever service a red Ford Bronco?"

"Yes, as a matter of fact, I do service John Badger's Ford Bronco. Why do you ask?"

"Just wanted to know if he was a customer of yours."

She giggled. "I thought you might want to meet him here and beat his ass again."

Dallas grinned. "I just might after some of the stories I've heard about him and his disrespect toward women and Mexican people. Do you know anything about him abducting a woman and showing her off, tied up like a deer on the top of an SUV?"

Lori's facial expression changed from a smile to a look of anger. "I heard about him and his buddies grabbing a young Mexican girl and driving around with her tied to the top of his SUV a month or so ago. I don't know if the story was true or not."

"I heard that Carlos intervened and freed the girl. Any truth to that?"

She quickly asked, "Who the hell are you, Dallas McCall?"

He chuckled. "I'm just that – Dallas McCall, a cowboy from Big Spring, Texas visiting friends."

Lori lowered her head and then raised up to look at Dallas. "Would you be interested in coming to my house for dinner tonight?" She looked away, her face flushed with embarrassment for being so straightforward.

A smile crossed Dallas's face. "I would like that. Thanks for asking. Where and what time?"

She smiled and handed him a personal card decorated with roses around the edges. "How about seven o'clock. The dress code is casual."

He glanced at the card. "Is this a country address?"

"It is, kinda of. It is easy to find. Just head out of town south; my house is the third house on the left from the city limits sign."

"Thanks. I'm off to the foothills to watch some more birds."

She laughed. "Yeah, right. Be careful. There are some dangerous birds out there. See you later."

Each time Dallas drove to Diablo Ridge, he felt that he was getting nearer to finding out who killed Carlos. It was a gut feeling that he had every time he read Carlos' last entry in his ledger the day he was murdered. *Carlos knew the person who pulled the trigger that day in August, and that person is running around free. The killer must have known that Carlos would be on the ridge that day, and what time he would be there. But how would anyone know except family or a close friend?*

It was nearly five o'clock as the sun cast long shadows over the foothills when Dallas started back to Little Creek. He remembered when he first met Carlos – five years back in Camp Lejeune, North Carolina. *Carlos was a newly promoted sergeant assigned to my team, and I could tell that he came from good family stock by the way he talked and followed orders. He was a good Marine and a good all-around good person and friend.*

Damn, Carlos was a tough man. He never backed down from a challenge or a direct order. As we went on many of missions together and worked closely with each other, our friendship grew, and we never had a problem with me being an officer and he an enlisted man. We were both modern-day cowboys serving our country and trying to survive to return home to our loved ones. I miss you, brother. Rest assured, you will never be forgotten.

Chapter 11

That evening, Dallas found Lori's house without difficulty after following the directions precisely as she told him. He parked the Jeep in the circular driveway next to the sidewalk leading up to a wide front porch. The outside light lit up the wicker table and chairs neatly arranged on the outdoor carpet of the porch. *Nice home. It looks better than anything I've seen around town so far. She must have some bucks.*

Lori answered the door, looking beautiful wearing a green dress, baring her shoulders and flowed out above her knees, showing her toned legs. Her red hair fell loosely around her shoulders.

"Right on time. Come in, please."

Dallas smiled. "Your directions were perfect." He handed Lori a six-pack of Corona beer in bottles. "Sorry, I couldn't find any wine or a flower shop in town."

She laughed. "You done good, I like beer. The town grocery store has wine, but it is cheap house wine. Come on in. I have margaritas mixed up. Would you like one before dinner?"

"Yes, I would, thanks. You sure have a nice home here." *That was a dumb thing to say before I've even seen the house.*

"Thank you. Why don't you come with me to the kitchen and I'll pour us a drink."

Dallas sat on a kitchen bar stool and watched Lori move around the stove and counter. He could not keep his eyes off of her as her back was toward him. *That woman has a great figure. I love that long red hair.*

Lori turned and smiled. "I hope you like spaghetti and meatballs, green garden salad and garlic bread?"

"You bet. One of my favorite meals. I like all types of Italian food. Hell, I like all food."

She laughed. "If you will excuse me, I will be right back." She picked up a tray with covered dishes and walked out of the kitchen and down the hallway toward the back of the house.

Dallas sat, quietly looking around at the modern and fully equipped kitchen. *Wonder who the tray of food is for. Maybe she has a man locked up in one of the bedrooms, and she plans to kidnap me and keep me as a sex slave. I would like that!* He laughed to himself.

Lori returned and slid down on the stool next to Dallas. "Since you are in my home, I owe you the courtesy of telling you about my life outside of running a garage and gas station. The tray of food I took was for my grandfather and grandmother that have a small flat in the rear of the house. They are 87 and 85 years old, and it is difficult for them to get around. They both use wheelchairs at times. I take care of them with the help of a Mexican woman who lives in town, Lupe. She stays with them during the daytime while I'm working at the garage. I prepare dinner, and we usually have our dinner together, but they insisted that they have dinner in their flat, so you and I could dine alone."

"You have your hands full, and you certainly have my respect. Being a young woman and managing a business along with the loving care of your grandparent's is remarkable. They sure would be welcome to join us for dinner if you would like them too."

"That's sweet of you. If you like, I will introduce you to them after dinner."

"I would like that."

Lori smiled and gently touched Dallas's arm. "Let's eat, I'm starved."

"Me too."

While eating dinner, Lori asked Dallas about his family in Texas. "My dad and mom are horse and cattle ranchers. The ranch is ten miles west of Big Spring, and they have 1,500 hundred acres that have been in the McCall family since 1875. I have one sister older than me who is married and teaches middle school in Big Spring. They have two little girls who are three and five."

She licked her lips and looked into his eyes. "So, you are a real cowboy?"

He grinned. "Well, yes, off and on. I went to Texas Tech for two years and got tired of sitting in a classroom, so I joined the Marines. I was a captain and resigned my commission in July of this year after eight years of active duty. That's about it for me!"

Lori smiled. "I think there is a lot more to you than that. The way you carry yourself and your mannerisms, I think you may be CIA."

He chuckled. "No, I am not CIA, FBI or a police detective. I'm just a man looking for the person or persons who killed my friend, Carlos. I owe him and his family that much."

"You are a good and loyal friend that's for sure."

"Okay, now that I've told you my life story, how about telling me about your double life?"

Lori laughed softly. "I do suppose I owe you that much. After I graduated from high school here in Little Creek, I attended New Mexico State University at Las Cruces on a scholarship. I graduated with a BA in Business Management and was hired by a large insurance agency in Las Cruces. During my second year of work, my parents were killed in an automobile accident outside of Albuquerque. My grandparents, who I am taking care of were hurt very bad, and their injuries left them crippled. I had no other choice than to return here and take care of my grandparents and take over Dad's garage business. That is what I have been doing for the past two years."

"Damn, that's terrible. I'm so sorry for your loss. Now I understand why you cut me off when I ask if you have a boyfriend or some other dumb question."

She smiled. "Now we can eliminate some of our questions about each other. You are a mysterious man – you know that, Dallas McCall?"

"I've been called worse than that. I want you to know up front that I think you are a beautiful, intelligent woman. I trust you."

"Thank you. In addition, I think you are an extremely handsome man. I like you mainly, well – because you are a real man. And I also trust you."

Their eyes connected and Lori reached for Dallas's hand. "I want you to know that I have not dated a man in four years so please excuse me if I am awkward and too forward."

"I like a woman who is straightforward. No bull crap or fake words being thrown around. As far as dating goes…I have not had time to date a woman since I returned home from Afghanistan."

Lori blurted out, "I guess we are both horny." Her face turned red, and she covered her mouth with her hand. "Oh, my God. I can't believe I said that to you."

They both broke out in laughter.

"Oh, my. Would you like some pie?"

They roared with laughter at Lori's unsuspected rhyming words.

"I'll have some pie," Dallas said, still laughing.

"Oh, my. I haven't laughed so hard in years. I'll get our pie. Would you like a cup of coffee?"

"Coffee will be fine, thanks."

A short time later, Lori introduced Dallas to her grandfather and grandmother Porter in their apartment at the rear of the house. They both had sharp minds and a good sense of humour. Dallas liked them, and from the vibes he got back from them, they also liked him.

Grandma Porter's eyes lit up, and she said, her voice trembling a little, held out her hand to Dallas. "What a tall fellow you are. Stand back, and let me look at you. Lori, that is a mighty handsome man you got there."

Dallas and Lori both blushed by her bold but loving remarks.

"Thank you, ma'am," Dallas replied.

"We must go now," Lori said. "I think this man is getting sleepy."

Dallas smiled and bid goodnight to Grandpa and Grandma Porter.

Lori walked with Dallas to the front door. They both stopped, and she stood on her tiptoes and kissed Dallas gently on the lips.

"We must continue this conversation if you were not scared off by Grandma," she said, her beautiful face was all smiles.

"Yes, we do. Thanks for the great meal, conversation and good company. I felt totally relaxed being with you. I enjoyed meeting your grandparents."

"Me too. I like being with you. Drop by the garage and see me." She kissed him again, slowly closed the door and bolted it.

She is a good woman, and I can tell she is loyal. I can never remember seeing a woman that beautiful with a dynamite body and so intelligent with common sense. When I complete my mission, I hope to spend more time with her. Nothing permanent, just being with her makes me happy. I am not ready to get involved and tied down. It would be a wise choice to be with Lori for the rest of my life, if she really loved me and understood me and my stubborn ways.

The drive back to the B&B was enough to cool him off and attempt to stop thinking about the beautiful redhead who aroused his manhood to the point of a near explosion.

Dallas unlocked the door, went into his room and turned on the light sitting behind the lone comfortable reclining chair. He thought about the enjoyable evening he had with Lori and how at ease he felt being with her.

His thoughts eventually changed to his mission in Little Creek and the obstacles he faced with his attempt to find Carlos's killer or killers.

Sleep wouldn't come until two o'clock when he finally drifted off to sleep into his world of nightmares.

Chapter 12

The morning sun seeping through the curtains in Dallas's room woke him from a tiresome sleep. *Damn nightmares will never go away.*

He ate breakfast at eight-thirty and scanned the Santa Fe newspaper that Mrs Norris laid on the table next to his coffee cup. He studied the paper and found nothing that interested him except that the United States military was still involved in Afghanistan. *My brothers and sisters are still in danger every day of being wounded or losing their lives. It's time to bring the troops home, Mister President.*

It was a little past nine o'clock that morning when he drove the Jeep toward the Garcia ranch, as he thought of a few more questions he wanted to ask Romon and Carla in person and not by a telephone call.

Carla was standing out on the porch, watching the sky toward the east and looking somewhat bored, while Christian was sitting on a chair in the corner of the porch helping his mother peel potatoes.

The distant sound of an automobile engine and a cloud of dust from the lane coming to their house caught Carla's attention. She raised up on her toes and placed her hand above her eyes to block out the rising sun. A smile formed across her mouth when she recognised the Jeep. "It's Dallas," she yelled out.

Christian jumped up from his chair and ran to the edge of the parking area with Carla trailing close behind him.

"Hey, Dallas, I am so happy to see you," Christian said meeting Dallas, as he climbed out of the driver's seat.

"Hey, little man, nice to see you too." He glanced over at Carla and her pretty, smiling face.

Dallas smiled at her. "Good morning, cowgirl. How are you doing this fine morning?"

"Good, I am much better seeing your handsome face." She was all smiles.

Dallas continued smiling. Their eyes met, and they stared at each other for a few seconds.

Romon came out of the house and stood by his wife, as Carla, Christian and Dallas walked up on the porch. Dallas and Romon exchanged handshakes; Dallas and Rosa smiled at each other.

"I hope you don't mind me stopping by unannounced? I have thought of a few questions that I hope you can clear up for me."

Romon replied. "You are always welcome at our home anytime you want. You are part of our family. Let's sit down and be more comfortable."

"I will bring out some coffee and pastries," Rosa said. She hurried in the house followed by Carla close behind her.

Rosa and Carla were back in no time sitting a tray filled with sweets, a coffee carafe and cups on the round table near the front door. Carla poured the coffee and then sat down in a chair beside Dallas.

Dallas took a sip of coffee. "That's good coffee, ma'am," he said grinning at Rosa.

"You said that you have more questions you want to ask?" Romon said.

"Yes, I do. I was wondering if Carlos had any close friends that still live around here?"

Carla chimed in on the conversation. "Yes, he and Diego Mendoza grew up together, and they were hunting and fishing buddies. Diego is two years younger than Carlos. You remember meeting his parents at our party. I think that they may have drifted apart when Carlos returned home from the Marines. Diego, in my opinion, he is very immature and spoiled by his parents."

"Oh, yeah. I liked them. You said their son, Diego and Carlos, may have had problems with each other."

"Yes. Diego is a good boy, but his father told me he seemed troubled since Carlos returned home from the Marines. He thought Diego might be jealous over all of the attention Carlos was getting from the younger people. That is understandable his father said, but he is acting very strange. Carlos never told me about any differences the two were having."

"Do you think the Mendozas would be offended if I paid them a courtesy visit?"

"No, not at all, they have always enjoyed having my family visit them," Carla replied. "I'm not busy this morning if you wanted to drive to the ranch. I would be happy to go with you."

"That would be great. I think that I will be more welcome in their home with you along. Are you free for an hour or so to go along with me?"

"Yes, I am. I'll grab us some water and be right back. Don't leave without me." She giggled.

As Dallas drove, he glanced over at Carla and admired her beauty. *Damn, she is a gorgeous woman. It's pretty difficult for a young man such as myself not to think about having an affair with her. I sure can't cause trouble between Lori and me. I need to distance myself from Carla. How in the hell am I going to do that and continue looking for Carlos's killer?*

"I love the early mornings," Carla sighed. "To me, the mornings are, stimulating."

"Me too. I have been getting up early every morning since I was a little boy growing up on our ranch. If I slept past seven o'clock in the morning, my day is shot."

"That's the road to the Mendoza ranch," Carla said, raising her hand and pointing ahead to her right.

Dallas turned the Jeep sharply to the right and began to descend down a long, narrow road built into the side of a steep, rocky bluff.

Below, they saw the ranch surrounded in green pastures along a valley that spread as far as they could see. To the west sprawled the house below, White Rock adobe style with broad porches and tall wide windows; further down the road, at the base of a gentle slope, were sheds, a high, round corrals and a large barn. Barbed-wire fences stretched away in all directions. A small creek, bordered with cottonwoods and scraggly willows, wound aimlessly away down the valley.

Dallas whistled through his teeth. "This is a state-of-the-art ranch. The family must be quite wealthy."

Carla replied. "Yes, they are rich but never talk about their cattle empire or how much land they own. They help out the smaller Mexican ranchers and never ask for anything in return."

Fifteen minutes later, Dallas pulled the Jeep to a stop in front of the ranch house. They were met by an older man wearing jeans, a blue work shirt and large sombrero along with a dark-brown Catahoula cow dog by his side.

"Hello, Jose," Carla said in Spanish. She switched to English. "This is my friend and a Marine friend of my brother, Carlos. Are the Senor and Senora at home?"

Jose looked over Dallas as he climbed out of the Jeep. "Si, he and the senora are inside the house. Come with me, please. I will take you to them."

They followed Jose as Carla walked beside Dallas. She said in a near whisper to Dallas, "Jose is the caretaker of the house. His wife is the housekeeper and cooks and cleans for the family. I think she also watched over Diego when he was a baby."

Dallas and Carla were met by the dashing figure of Miguel Mendoza, as they entered the large open living room. His arms wide open, he embraced Carla and smiled at Dallas.

"Welcome, young man. It is nice to see you again." He reached his right hand to Dallas.

Dallas extended his hand to Miguel. "Thank you, sir. I am pleased to see you again. Please excuse us for coming unannounced. Carla's father said you would welcome us."

"Of course. You are always welcome at our home. Ivanna will be out to greet you in a minute. Please, let's be seated." Miguel opened the palm of his hand toward the brown leather couches and chairs sitting in front of a massive stone fireplace.

Just as they were seated, Ivanna walked into the room moving gracefully to Carla where she hugged her and then extended her hand to Dallas, as he stood to meet her. "Please, be seated." She sat down on a couch next to her husband facing Dallas and Carla.

Dallas thought about Ivanna's soft hand touching his hand and their eyes meeting for a split second. *I can't get over how beautiful Ivanna is. Miguel is a lucky man to be married to such a gorgeous woman.*

A slightly plump Mexican woman entered the room carrying a tray filled with a stainless steel coffee craft, white porcelain cups and a plate of cookies.

Ivanna poured the coffee and passed a plate of cookies to everyone. "What brings you two out this way today?" she asked, her voice soft and gentle.

Dallas glanced at Carla. *I am going to lie to them so I can find out more about their son.* "I wondered if I could meet your son, Diego? Carlos told me a lot about the two of them when they were growing up. I just would like to put a face with the name for my memories of my friend."

Ivanna smiled. "Yes, they were good friends when they were little cowboys and when they were in school. Carlos was two grades ahead of Diego. Diego is so heartbroken by the death of Carlos and has not been the same boy since that horrible day. He is in his room; I will ask him to come and meet you." She excused herself and walked out of the room.

Miguel said, "Have you heard if the sheriff has found any suspects or any clues as to who murdered Carlos?"

Carla answered before Dallas could speak. "No, not yet. We think he does not have enough deputies to help him. We have not given up hope, and we support the sheriff in his investigation."

Dallas quickly glanced at Carla as she spoke. *She is trying to protect me by not letting Miguel, and his wife knows I am investigating the murder.*

Ivanna returned to the room followed by a slender dark-haired handsome young man with the beginning of a beard on his face. He wore faded jeans and a black T-shirt. He was barefooted.

"This is our son, Diego," Ivanna said, her hand on his shoulder. "Son, this is Mr Dallas McCall, a Marine friend of Carlos."

Diego nodded his head but made no attempt to shake hands with Dallas or make eye contact. He turned his head and smiled at Carla.

He damn sure has an attitude. He's nothing like his parent's. Dallas, with a fake smile on his face, cordially said, "Nice to meet you, Carlos spoke highly of you and your friendship."

Diego still did not make eye contact with Dallas. He turned his head to his mother. "I've got to get ready for my trip to Santa Fe," he said in Spanish. Without looking at his father, Carla or Dallas, he turned and walked swiftly out of the room and down the long hallway.

His parent's appeared to be embarrassed by their son's rudeness. Miguel said, "Please excuse him. He has not been the same since Carlos was murdered. We don't know what to do for him except for him to work out his problems himself."

Dallas turned his head to Carla. "We should be going and let these people go on with their day."

"Yes, we should go." She and Dallas raised up from the couch. Carla hugged Ivanna and Miguel, and Dallas exchanged handshakes.

"Thank you for the coffee and hospitality," Dallas said as they all walked toward the massive wooden double front entrance doors.

"Please, come back anytime and visit us you two," Miguel said. "We hope next time Diego will feel better and he can visit with you."

As they drove away from the ranch, Dallas asked Carla, "Did Carlos and Diego really get along other than what you have already told me?"

"Well, as I told you before, they did when they were younger but when Carlos joined the Marines, Diego was…was kind of jealous with all their friends wanting to hang around with Carlos. When he got home from the Marines, Diego never came over to the ranch or hung out with Carlos as he did before. We heard he was tagging along with Ty Denton, John Badger and Weasel."

Dallas sat without speaking as he drove thinking about how Diego acted toward him. *He may know something about Carlos' murder, or he may be mentally disturbed.*

"What are you thinking about?" Carla asked. "Oh, I know. You are thinking about me." She giggled.

"Yep, I was wondering how you put on those tight jeans."

She playfully hit him on the shoulder. "Wouldn't you like to know!"

He smiled at the soft sound of her voice. "Yes, I would."

Carla started to say something, but no words came from her mouth.

"Did you say something?" Dallas asked.

"Oh, never mind." She turned in her seat and looked away at the passing landscape.

I wonder what was on her mind? A man never knows what a woman is thinking. That's what makes them so unique.

"Appreciate you coming with me today to the Mendozas. Their son is a weird kid; he's nothing like his parents."

Carla replied, "No, he is not anywhere near like them. He has changed since he was a little boy. He is troubled about something."

Back at the ranch, Dallas said goodbye to the Garcias and accepted their invitation to return for a meal anytime that he wanted.

Carla walked with him to the Jeep. She looked up at Dallas; a sly smile appeared on her lips. "I miss you and hope you come back soon."

"I miss you too. I promise that my next visit will be soon." Before he climbed in the Jeep, Carla raised up on her toes and kissed him on the lips.

Dallas, with a surprised look said, "Adios, pretty woman."

She turned and quickly ran back to the porch. She stopped before entering the house, turned and watched Dallas as he drove away down the lane. *I'll see you later, Mr McCall. You can bet your cowboy boots on that!*

As Dallas cruised the familiar road back to Little Creek, he wondered if the kiss she gave him was in friendship or was she making a move on him. *Be careful, McCall. You can't take the chance of getting involved with your dead friend's sister. She is a beautiful, young woman and hard to resist. Maybe after this is all over, I will feel differently about our relationship. I have my whole life ahead of me, and I sure don't want to make a bad choice and miss out on loving a good woman and her loving and respecting me for me. Crap, McCall. You thought the same way about Lori. You're going to hell for sure.* He shook his head in disgust at the way he felt about the two special women in his life know that one of them would be chosen and the other one heartbroken and pissed off. *Maybe I should leave them both alone and when I finish my mission, get on the train and go on back to Texas.*

Chapter 13

It was a little past one o'clock on Wednesday afternoon when Dallas stopped the Jeep alongside the gas pumps at Lori's garage.

"Hello there, stranger," came the sweet voice of Lori walking up behind him.

"Hello yourself, pretty woman."

He turned to find her standing close to him, almost touching his body, a warm smile on her pretty face.

"I've missed you, cowboy."

Dallas grinned. "Yes, me too. Let's see... It's been about fourteen or fifteen hours since we last saw each other. I think you're just after the Jeep rental money I pay you."

She laughed softly. "Fourteen to fifteen hours. That's too long. No, I'm not after your hard-earned money. Have you been out in the foothills looking at birds again?"

Dallas placed the nozzle back on the pump and tightened the gas cap on the Jeep. "Yes, I have – birds that don't fly." He inched his hips to touch Lori's hips, and he quietly asked, "Do you know much about Diego Mendoza?"

"No, I really don't know very much about him except what I've heard. I have only seen him occasionally. Why do you ask?" She bumped her hips to his and smiled.

"I met him today, and he was rude as hell."

"So, you were at the Mendoza ranch, were you? Who showed you the way, Carla Garcia?" She shook her head and gave him a sassy look.

Dallas grinned, "Yes, Carla went with me." He decided not to add fuel to the fire, as he thought Lori might be a little bit jealous.

Lori looked closely at Dallas, and then a smile spread across her face. "I was about ready to grab some lunch; you want to join me?"

"You bet. I'm hungry. I'll drive."

"Give me a minute while I get rid of these coveralls and wash up."

Within minutes, she returned from inside and jumped into the passenger seat. "Head up the main street toward town. How about the M&J?"

He laughed, "Duh, that's the only restaurant in town."

Heads turned when Dallas and Lori walked in the front door of the restaurant. Dallas saw the men's eyes watching Lori go past them wearing tight jeans and a tight fitting white blouse.

They took a seat at a corner table. Dallas sat in a chair with his back to the wall. He saw Ty Denton and a blonde haired young woman seated at a table in front of them.

Ty shot glances at Dallas and Lori. The girl whispered to Ty, and they quickly turned their heads again toward Lori and Dallas.

Lori, sitting to the right of Dallas caught Ty's awkward glances at them. She said quietly, "I think Ty is checking you out. He probably is afraid that you are going to beat his ass as you did to his buddy, John Badger."

"Naw, he's looking at you and can't figure out what you are doing with the stranger in his town."

"Yeah, right. Have you ever formally met him?"

"No. I want to, but it will be on my terms."

A sober-faced older woman stood in front of the table to take their food order. "Our special today is beef stew," she rattled off.

"No, thanks. We will order from the menu," Lori said.

Fifteen minutes later, the waitress sat down a garden salad and a tall glass of iced tea in front of Lori and a green chili cheeseburger, fries and iced tea for Dallas.

"Anything else?" she asked.

"Nope, you've been more than kind," Dallas replied back without making eye contact. He looked at Lori and raised his eyebrows.

She put her hand on her mouth to keep from laughing out loud. "You're bad!"

They talked quietly and laughed while they ate. Lori was playing knees with Dallas, and he liked it.

Ty continued with his sly glances at Dallas and Lori. She caught Ty looking at her, and then he sheepishly looked away.

When they finished eating, Dallas placed the money for their meals on the table, and they moved towards the front door. As they passed the table where Ty and the woman sat, Dallas stopped next to Ty and glared down at him.

"We still need to talk, Denton. You're gonna get a sore neck sneaking looks at us. Y'all have a nice day, hear!" Dallas gently took hold of Lori's arm and guided her out of the restaurant.

As they drove away, Lori said, "Well, I guess you got Ty's attention. You will never get him alone to talk to him. There is someone with him at all times. Even when he was in high school, one or more of friends were always with him."

"I'll find the opportunity to have a talk with him. I'm to the point now where I want to speak to his father before I speak to Ty."

Lori reached over and placed her hand on his arm. "I wish you luck with your search for whoever killed Carlos, but I'm afraid you will never get the support of the sheriff or the local people. I have no more information for you, but I'll pay close attention when I hear the townspeople gossiping."

"Thanks, pretty lady. I will never give up my mission of finding the people who ambushed and killed Carlos. I owe it to him and his family."

Dallas stopped the Jeep in front of the door going to the garage office. "See you later, sooner than later," he said.

She smiled. "Sooner, I hope. I would love to spend more time with you. We have more to talk about."

"I would like that. You know I spend most of my days exploring the open prairies and mountains and my nights at the local B&B lying awake in my empty room. My excitement in life is when I'm with you."

"Really! How about if I fix us a picnic basket, and we drive out to a spot I know in the mountains. My old faithful employee Jose will hold down the garage while I am away."

"You got yourself a date, baby. Where and what time should I pick you up in – your Jeep?"

She laughed, "The Jeep is more yours than mine. How about nine o'clock in the morning at my house. We can get an early start and enjoy the morning and a long day together. Are you sure that you want to be alone with me for a day?"

Dallas laughed, "Yes, of course; you're on."

"See you tomorrow." She leaned over and kissed him on his cheek, jumped out of the passenger seat and disappeared inside the garage office.

On the way back to the B&B, Dallas looked for Ty Denton's pickup along the town streets. The truck was nowhere in sight. *He must have gone back to his daddy's ranch. I'll find him alone and have a little one-on-one chat with him.*

He glanced at his watch. 2:45. *I'll take a ride up to Diablo Ridge and see what I can dig up. There is always a hidden clue in a murder case – So I have been told!*

Dallas drove steadily over the rough, rocky road on his way to Diablo Ridge. Tall cliffs were on the left side of the Jeep and on the right was a deep drop off down to the valley below. He rounded a sharp curve and glanced in the side mirror. He saw a white pickup truck following close behind him; the windshield was tinted, but he made out the images of two people in the cab.

After another glance in the mirror, the truck was only a few feet from the rear of the Jeep. He quickly glanced over his shoulder, and by the erratic way, the driver was manoeuvring the truck, he knew that he was being chased. *This Jeep is no match for that truck. I need to find a place to pull off and let those assholes pass me.*

His eyes moved to the side mirror, and now the truck looked like it was inches from the rear of the Jeep. Dallas raised his right hand up giving them the middle finger gesture and then he clinched his fist and shook it.

Dallas felt a rush of adrenaline kick in as he fought to contain control of the Jeep as it skidded around sharp turns. The road dropped sharply into a steep incline; on the right, he saw the drop off below with a few inches of the road to his left. His eyes caught a glimpse of a narrow path going off the side of the road on his left. Fighting for control of the veering Jeep Dallas turned sharply into the rocky path and slammed on the brakes coming to an abrupt stop the front of the Jeep against a large boulder.

The truck passed by where the Jeep was stopped and Dallas saw the brake lights go on. The truck stopped, and the driver started to back up the road toward where Dallas was parked.

Dallas, tired and pissed off pulled his pistol out from his holster and fired three rapid shots at the tailgate of the truck. The roar of the engine and rocks thrown in the air by the dual tires from the fleeing pickup filled the mountain air.

I got you now, you sorry son of a bitch. A white Ford 350 dually with three bullet holes in the tailgate. That truck should be easy to find.

Dallas backed the Jeep out from between the rocks and onto the road. *I've had enough excitement for today.* He drove back down the road toward Little Creek talking himself out of trying to find the white truck. *If I saw the people who were in the truck, I would probably shoot them. I need answers. Dead men don't talk.* He took two pain pills and tried to ignore the pain in his leg.

Chapter 14

Thirty minutes later while driving up the main street of Little Creek returning to the B&B, Dallas spotted a white Ford dually pickup parked in front of the Little Creek Tavern. *Oh, crap. Now I got to find out who that truck belongs to while I am still pissed off. Keep your cool, McCall; don't go shooting people and end up in jail. You can't help Carlos that way.*

He swung the Jeep around and stopped behind the white truck and climbed out of the driver's seat and walked up to the rear of the truck. He saw three bullet holes the size of his index finger. *Nice shootin', McCall, a three-inch spread between the holes on a moving target. Your old Marine Corps small arm's instructor would be proud of you.*

Dallas entered the tavern and immediately heard the loud horse laugh of John Badger rising above the crowd. Sitting at a table near the wall sat Badger, Weasel and a Mexican man wearing a tan baseball cap with a large green deer emblem on the front.

Wasting no time, Dallas moved directly to the table where the three sat smoking cigarettes and drinking bottled beer.

"Who owns the white Ford dually parked in front?" Dallas stood rigidly and glared at the men who were exchanging glances with each other.

The man wearing the ballcap said without looking at Dallas, "I own the truck. What about it?"

Dallas inched forward toward the man who now raised his head to look at him.

"You tried to run me off of the road up in the mountains a short time ago, and I don't appreciate it a damn bit."

"You should take some driving lessons on how to drive on mountain roads," the man wearing the hat said with a smirk on his face.

Dallas took a quick step forward, and with lightning speed, he grabbed the corner of the table and turned it upside down causing the three occupants to fall from their chairs on the dirty wood floor, the table laying on top of them.

The Mexican man started to get up on his feet, but a swift hard kick to his ribcage from the toe of Dallas's boot sent him back to the floor where he laid wrenching in pain. Dallas said in a loud, angry voice, "You will find three bullet holes in the tailgate of your truck. If you take a look at the shot group, you will know that I'm an expert marksman. Stay away from me…this is your final warning. If you want to file a complaint against me, go ahead. I could care less. I'm warning you again. If any of you were involved with the death of Carlos Garcia, beware – I'm coming for your sorry asses." With a quick turn, Dallas walked out of the tavern without looking back.

Ty Denton wasn't with his friends today. Maybe I have him all wrong! I'm still looking for the right opportunity to speak with him and his father.

Dallas returned to his room and took a long hot shower trying to calm himself down so that he could plan his next move.

After drying off and putting on his sleeping clothes, he flopped down in the recliner, and after a couple of beers, he closed his eyes and drifted off to sleep. He woke up at eight o'clock, ate a sandwich and laid down in his bed. Sleep finally came, and he entered his world of nightmares.

It was a crisp sunny Thursday morning, when Dallas drove into the driveway at Lori's house. She scrambled out of the front door of the house with a big smile on her face carrying a wicker basket and a chrome thermos jug. She was dressed in jeans and boots, and she wore a tan jacket that fell to her hips, and a blue denim shirt tucked inside of her jeans.

Dallas took the basket and thermos from her and placed them behind the passenger seat. Lori hopped in the Jeep and kissed Dallas on the cheek. "Hey, cowboy. You are punctual as usual."

He smiled, "You look beautiful this morning… I mean beautiful as always."

She laughed, "Yeah, you say that to all the women you pick up in your sexy Jeep."

"You know that's not so. Where are we going?"

Lori motioned with her right hand. "Towards the south on Ranch Road 24 to the southern foothills. Have you been out that way yet?"

"Nope, this will be my first time. What's special out there?"

She grinned and tossed her head to the side. "It is a special place that I found when I was a teenager out exploring with a girlfriend. You will like it."

Dallas guided the Jeep south over the winding ranch road noticing the changing landscape from the southern side of the mountains.

After nearly an hour, Lori pointed off to the right and shouted over the sound of the wind blowing through the open sides of the Jeep. "There is a narrow road just ahead on the right; turn there."

Dallas followed a winding road up to a bluff, and then the road ended. "We will hike from here just a short distance over the top of the rocks." Dallas grabbed the picnic basket from the Jeep, and Lori carried the thermos.

Upon reaching the top, Lori, who was walking in the lead, stopped. She turned and smiled as Dallas joined her. "Well, what do you think of this?" She extended her right arm out and moved it from her left to right.

He moved his head and eyes slowly looking out into the valley. "My lord, what a breath-taking view of the surrounding streams and woodlands. This is really very beautiful, and it is so quiet and peaceful here."

Lori crunched up her shoulders and smiled. "Wait until you see the special surprise I have for you. Follow me, cowboy."

It was a short walk over a rocky path and up a slope along the edge of the green forest. Lori turned to Dallas walking close behind her. "Were here."

Dallas moved up and stood beside Lori. In front of them were three hot springs pools scenically arranged within the trees in a mountain meadow.

"This is the closest thing nature has to a sauna," she said, excitement in her voice. "Do you like it?"

Dallas nodded his head. "What is there not to like about a picturesque place like this." He moved his head and eyes around and a smile formed on his face. "This is the perfect place to skinny dip."

"So, I've been told. I've never done that before." Her face reddened, and she moved to a location near the springs and sat down the thermos. "I have a blanket in the basket we can spread out to sit on while we eat lunch."

Dallas laughed as he looked at his watch. 10:30. "It's kinda' early for lunch."

Lori turned her head to face him. "Oh, well we can eat when we are ready then, can't we?"

Around an hour later, they sat and munched on fried chicken and talked about life in the small town of Little Creek and the secrets that were hidden by the people who live there. Lori stared at the hot steam coming from the tops of the springs. She turned her head to face Dallas. "Do you have any idea what so ever who might have killed Carlos?"

"Yes and no. There are a couple of people I suspect and on the other hand… I don't have enough evidence or a reason why anyone would want Carlos dead. When I find that out, then I will know who and why he was murdered."

"I know how you must be hurting inside by losing your close friend. I only wish that I could help you more."

Dallas, who was lying on his side on the blanket, reached over and placed his hand on Lori's hand. "Have you ever been in the water of the springs?"

"Yes, a couple of times when my girlfriend and I were here. The water is hot but not enough to burn. You want to test the water?"

He jumped to his feet, reached down and pulled Lori up to his side. "Did you bring a bathing suit?"

"No, did you?" she answered laughing.

"Well, no. I had no idea we would go swimming. I do have underwear on." His smile was continuous.

"Truthfully, I have never said or done this before with a man. I will strip down to my panties and bra; that is about the same as a two-piece bathing suit, isn't it?"

"Roger that." He sat back down on the blanket and removed his boots, pulled off his jeans, unbuttoned his shirt and stood in front of Lori wearing black jockey underwear. "I'm ready."

Lori's eyes were glued to his muscular, tanned body, memorising every inch of him. She noticed a large scar that resembled a zipper running about six-inches down his right hip. *That must be the wound that causes him to limp.*

She slowly removed her boots, jeans, jacket and shirt and stood to face Dallas wearing a white bra that was filled with full breasts and white bikini panties. "Well, I'm ready to test the water."

He took her hand in his, and they carefully made their way over the rocks to the edge of the nearest pool of water.

Dallas went directly into the water and stopped when the water covered his waist. *I needed to get into the water fast before Lori saw how aroused I am. Damn what a body that woman has.*

Lori joined him and moved her arms around making waves. "This feels like being in a large hot tub. Is the water too hot for you?"

"No, I'm fine. There probably is a drop off near the middle. Have you been over to the other side?"

"Yes, I remember walking around in here this spring. I think it must be fairly level. Are you a good swimmer?"

Dallas replied, "Yeah, pretty good. I was a Marine Raider, and swimming was a requirement. I have been swimming since I was three years old."

"I love to swim, but there are no swimming pools in Little Creek. Can you imagine that; a town without a city or park pool?"

"I feel sorry for the kids in town not having a cement pool. They can swim in the nearby river, but that is not always safe."

Lori said bluntly, "Do you mind if I go topless?"

"No, no," Dallas quickly replied. A sheepish grin crossed his face.

She removed her bra and threw in on the rocks. She then bent her body down into the water and came back up with her panties in her hand. She threw them near her bra. Cocking her head smiling, she said, "Well, I'm ready to skinny dip. Why don't you join me?"

Dallas had his underwear off in seconds and threw them on the nearby rocks. "Okay, now what do you want to do?"

Within seconds, they were tangled up in each other's arms, their bodies melted together as one. They made love over and over again in the water before lying naked on the blanket feeling the warm autumn sun on them and gazing into each other's eyes.

"That was amazing," Lori said, as she laid her head on Dallas's chest.

"It sure was. You are quite the woman and a tiger in disguise." He kissed her, and she moved her body on top of his.

An hour later, Lori whispered in Dallas's ear, "I hate to tell you, but we should be going back to my house."

Dallas kissed her. "If you say so. We will continue this later."

Lori smiled and kissed him on his neck and then his lips. "Yes, we will, and soon."

On the drive back to Lori's house, she and Dallas exchanged smiles and glances at each other. Lori blew him a kiss, and he almost lost control of the Jeep watching her tease him rolling her tongue over her lips.

In her driveway, Lori climbed out of the passenger seat with the help of Dallas. She put her arms around his neck. "What a great day I had, thank you so much for sharing my secret location with me. I will never forget our lovemaking; it was heavenly."

Dallas with a broad grin on his mouth, replied, "Those are the words a man wants to hear after making love with a beautiful, loving woman. You are an exceptional lady."

Tears formed in her eyes. "You make me feel so special. I have never felt the way for a man as I do for you. I feel…well; I feel wanted and safe when I'm with you. I could make love with you forever."

"I feel the same way. I don't want you to get mixed up with my investigation. There are some dangerous people out there, and they are probably people you may know."

"I am not afraid of any of the trash in town. They have no reason to hurt me. I am afraid for you! I know that you can take care of yourself but so could Carlos, and he was ambushed and murdered by cowards."

Dallas pulled her to him and kissed her on her waiting lips. "You just be careful, you hear?" he whispered.

"Yes, sir. I had better get inside as it is time for my grandparent's caretaker to go home." She kissed him and hurried off to the front porch. Lori turned and waved at Dallas before going inside the house.

As he drove away, he could not stop thinking about the 5 foot 6-inch slender, red-haired beauty. *She is a keeper…that's for sure. We are getting a little too close to each other. I'm letting my guard down, and that is dangerous with what I am doing. Another old saying goes; a penis has no conscious! Back off, McCall and give yourself space to do what you came here to do.*

When Dallas returned to his room, he grabbed a beer from the fridge and sat down in the recliner. He called his mother in Texas to find out if his family was doing all right.

"We are all good. We miss you; when are you coming home?"

"Soon, mom, I hope. I am enjoying being with Carlos's family and meeting their friends." He never told his family that he was hunting for the people responsible for Carlos's murder.

"You take care of yourself and make sure you eat good food. Your dad sends his love, and he misses you."

"I love you both. Don't worry about me. Talk to you soon." He disconnected the call.

He wrote on stationary lying on the desk notes for plans tomorrow. He wrote:

– Pay a visit to Sheriff Dan Baker and find out where he is at on the investigation.

– Take another look around Diablo Ridge to look for anything that I may have missed.

– Keep an eye out for Carlos's ledger.

Chapter 15

It was Friday morning around ten o'clock when Dallas entered the office of Sheriff Dan Baker.

Dan was alone, and he looked up from his desk as Dallas walked toward where he sat behind a pile of folders and empty plastic water bottles scattered around.

"Hey Sheriff, you have a minute?" Dallas asked.

"Sure, what's on your mind?"

Dallas sat down in the chair the sheriff pointed to. "How are you coming along with the Carlos Garcia murder investigation?"

"We've not found any new evidence nor do we have a suspect or suspects. This appears to be an old west type ambush. You know; the bad guy shoots the good guy from a hidden location and rides away without any witnesses."

Dallas sat rigid in the chair staring at the sheriff. "Maybe it's about time you got some outside help since you seem to be getting nowhere."

"If I requested assistance, it would take weeks, maybe months before assistance would be approved. Since this is a county case and not federal, I doubt that I could never receive support from the state."

Dallas stiffened in his chair. "Me not being a law enforcement official find that hard to believe. If I can provide you with a suspect, would you interrogate that person?"

"Yes, of course, I would. That is the law."

Dallas relaxed and leaned back in the chair. "Even if it was one of the good ole' boys in your county?"

The sheriff glared at Dallas. "Hell yes, I will interrogate any person suspected of any crime in my county, as long as there is evidence to support the questioning. I don't know where you are going with this Mr McCall, but if you're indicating that I am turning a blind eye to this case to cover up for local people, you are sadly mistaking."

Dallas thought over what Dan told him and the tone in his voice and the hardness of his eyes. He grinned, "No, I don't believe you would, sheriff. I want no trouble from the law, especially you. I only wanted to make sure that I could trust you. And, I believe that I can."

The sheriff moved his head and shoulders forward and placed both hands on the top of his desk and looked directly into the eyes of Dallas. "I trust you; I always have since we first met. I can use your help in an unofficial capacity. How about us teaming unofficially, and find the people who were responsible for murdering your friend?"

"That's the best damn news I've heard since I got off of the train a couple of weeks ago. I'm pretty damn deep in this investigation. I'm in. Where would you like to start?"

The sheriff reached his right hand to Dallas. Dallas gripped his hand, and the two former Marines were bonded by their word.

Dan said, "I'm going to begin questioning the men hanging around town that should be working and not loitering. I've made a plea for anyone with information about the killing to come forward. Would you go up to Diablo Ridge and take another close look around? We may have missed something during our investigation. My two deputies will return to duty tomorrow. They've been attending a training course in Santa Fe. This will give us two more investigators."

Dallas raised his long body from his chair. "That's just what I was planning to do. I know you are relieved to have your deputies back on duty. See you later." He rose up from the chair and walked out of the office.

During the drive to Diablo Ridge, Dallas knew that he needed to find out if anyone had a grudge against Carlos that was strong enough to kill him. *If we could only find his ledger; where did you hide it, my friend? I will never stop looking for your killer or killers. I will search until I find the ledger, and when I do, I will make the cowards pay for taking you away from your family and friends.*

Dallas parked the Jeep and walked straight to where Carlos' body was found. He kneeled down on one knee and moved his head around scanning the rocky terrain. *By what the Garcia family told me, Carlos' body was found behind his ATV facing this way.* He raised his arm and pointed. *His wounds were all in the front of his body. It's possible he knew who shot him, and he was ambushed from the rocks up above.*

He laid down on his back taking the position; he thought Carlos was lying in when he was killed. *If he had his ledger with him, he might have thrown it away to prevent whoever was shooting him from finding it.*

The edge of the ridge was to the right side of where Dallas laid. *Carlos may have tossed the ledger that way without being seen.* He got to his feet and walked back to the top of the ridge; looked down and evaluated the possibilities of climbing down the rocky area below. *Yeah, I can do it. I did it many times in the Mountains of Afghanistan.*

Using his military training skills, Dallas slowly and carefully descended down the side of the ridge keeping his eyes peeled on the rocks around him for the possibility of finding the missing ledger.

He continued to move slowly down the side of the Rocky Ridge looking in clumps of bushes growing out of the rocks in hopes of finding the ledger that may have entries that will lead-up to the time of Carlos' death. He was about to give up and climb back to the top of the ridge when out of the corner of his eyes, he spotted what looked like a sandwich ziplock bag. Moving over to his left, he moved two small rocks aside and removed the bag. Inside, he removed a small tablet or book. It was Carlos' ledger!

Dallas hesitated and then removed a rubber band from the cover and stared at the writing on the first page. He recognised the near perfect penmanship of Carlos and sorted through the details of what might have been his last hours alive. He took two pain pills washing them down with water from the bottle in his jacket pocket and then read the entries, beginning with his current entry first.

It was dusk on August 5, Sunday when I rode my ATV from the ridge heading down the rocky trail to our ranch in the valley below. I rode up to my favorite spot, Diablo Ridge, early that morning to check for stray cattle that wandered off from the main herd looking for grass in the foothills.

Only last month, I was a combat Marine in Afghanistan serving my second tour since enlisting four years ago. I loved the Marine Corps, but the love of my family and the New Mexico vast prairies and mountains called me home.

I hope my buddy from Texas keeps his promise and visits my family and me. He would love it up here from what he told me about him growing up on a ranch in West Texas. I mailed his letter this morning, so maybe he will give me a call. I sure hope so, he was a top-notch Marine, and his rank of captain never let it go to his head. We got to know each other on all of our recon patrols.

I brought the ATV to a halt halfway down the rocky path along the ridge when I spotted something off to my right. The sun had almost disappeared over the mountains and throwing reflections on the rocks.

I dismounted the ATV and moved toward where I saw the movement. Without warning, I heard a loud explosive sound of a rifle being fired echoing through the late-afternoon air. A bullet hit me in the left leg. It must have come from a rifle with a scope to shoot me from where I was hiding. I see a figure coming toward me; a person dressed in camouflage firing shots at me. Last entry. I need to get rid of this. I love you, Mom, Dad, Carla and Christian.

He flipped through the pages and glanced at entries going back to July after he was discharged from the Marines. Dallas placed the ledger in the pocket of his jeans and climbed back to the top of the ridge. He sat in the driver's seat of the Jeep and opened the ledger and began reading more of Carlos' entries.

Thursday, August 2: Diego Mendoza dropped by the ranch when I was working on corral fences. I had only seen him once since I got home. He told me that he overheard John Badger bragging about how he was going to run all of us Mexicans out of the county; especially the Garcia family and get rid of me who is causing us problems. Diego went on to say our land was worth ten times more than what we thought it was worth. He also said something about a developer wanted to use the properties for recreational ranches. I thanked Diego and asked him if he wanted to go hunting with me when deer season opens. He agreed and then, he left. That made me feel better, since he had been avoiding me since I came back home. There was talk that he was jealous of me and I was taking all of his friends away from him. That is not true.

Tuesday, July 31: I was coming out of the feed store when I saw tied to the top of John Badger's Ford Bronco was a woman. I made her out to be a young-looking Mexican woman wearing a yellow dress that was torn and dirty. She was crying. Four men got out of the vehicle; the driver was John Badger, and then I saw Weasel, and then I saw a man get out of the rear seat. I had never seen him before. He was a Mexican. Then Ty Denton came out of the hotel, and he began shaking hands with the other three, and they were laughing and pointing at the woman tied to the vehicle. I could see her trying to move her hands. I couldn't stand by and watch the girl suffer. I walked up to the Bronco and cut the woman loose and helped her down, and I told her to get the hell out of here. She began running down the street toward the west. I walked around to where the four men were standing with their backs to the vehicle and me. They were not aware that I had freed the woman. I grabbed John Badger by the neck of his shirt and threw him to the pavement. The other three men turned quickly staring at me. The man who I did not recognise stepped toward me and I knocked him to the ground. I shook my fist at Ty Denton and Weasel. Denton yelled out, I might kill you for this. I paid no attention to what he said and turned and walked across the street and got into my truck and drove away back to the ranch.

Thursday, July 19: In the bank, I overheard talk between Bill Denton, his son, Ty and two men dressed in fancy suits. I found out they were a land developer from Santa Fe wanting to buy up the land and build hunting clubs and dude ranches. They said, the big ranchers are too powerful and are financially able to decline the high stakes offers. However, the smaller ranches mainly owned by Mexican-American families are barely making ends meet. Their families have been landowners longer than most of the Anglo ranch owners. They did not see me.

Monday, July 16: Little Creek: I got into a big fight with two of the cowboys and beat the crap out of them. Their ranch manager, the owner's son, Ty Denton and two no accounts threatened to kill me and burn down my folk's ranch. I told them.

Come near my family, and I will put a 30.30. bullet in your ugly face. That didn't go over so good.

Dallas closed the ledger and placed it in the back pocket of his jeans. *John Badger and Ty Denton are the prime suspects the way I see it so far. I don't want to interfere with the sheriff's investigation. I will pass the information in the ledger to him.*

When Dallas got back in town, he stopped by the sheriff's office and informed him that he had found Carlos's ledger. Dan made copies and placed them in the official police evidence and investigation folder.

"Good job," Dan said. "We are getting closer every day to finding out who murdered Carlos."

"I hope so. Is this normal for a small town murder case to be so difficult?"

Dan nodded. "Yes, since people in smaller towns do not want to get involved with such a crime as murder. They keep their secrets to themselves and go on living their daily lives and close their blinds and lock their windows and doors after dark."

"I never thought of it that way until I arrived here. You gotta respect their loyalty, but on the other hand, they are living life behind closed doors."

"You hit the nail on the head. You want a deputy sheriff job?"

"Oh, no. I got to run. See you later, sheriff." Dallas grinned on the way out.

As Dallas drove toward the B&B, his cell phone buzzed. He glanced at the screen, and it showed, Private Caller.

He took the call. "This is McCall."

A voice came through the receiver that Dallas did not recognise. The voice was muffled and sounded like it was coming from out of doors, as he heard the wind blowing.

"McCall, get out of Little Creek and never come back. You are not wanted here and your time is nearing an end. We know where your Mexican friends and your pretty girlfriend live. No more warnings."

"You spineless bastard. You're too much of a coward to face me," he yelled in the phone.

The phone call was disconnected by the unknown caller.

Dallas banged his fist on the steering wheel of the Jeep and yelled; "Now you've really got me pissed off."

He gave a quick phone call to Carla and told her to be extra cautious if Bill Denton or any investors came on their property. He never told her about the threatening phone call, as he did not want to alarm her just warn her to be careful.

He called Lori and told her he would see her tomorrow. "I'm going to rest my body tonight and hope to get a good night's sleep."

"Please do, I know you are worn out. Sleep tight and dream about me."

Dallas laughed, "If I dreamed about you, I never would get any sleep."

Chapter 16

Saturday, October 13

Dallas woke up earlier than usual the next morning after another sleepless night. He was not refreshed, and he was still exhausted.

He was ready to go downstairs for breakfast when he noticed an envelope lying on the bottom inside of the room door. He picked it up and saw his name on the outside. He ripped it open and removed a folded sheet of white bond paper and read the contents printed in black ink. *Meet me at Diablo Ridge today at 12 o'clock. I have information for you.*

He laughed softly. *Yeah right. Probably a long gun with scope pointed at my back. What the hell. I've got to go, this may prove to be interesting!*

Dallas asked Mrs Norris if she left the note under the door to his room.

She replied, "No. Maybe the housekeeper left it."

All sorts of thoughts ran through Dallas's mind as he drove along the lonely curvy road to meet an unknown contact that may, in fact, be the person who killed Carlos. *Guess I will find out real soon!*

It was high noon when Dallas arrived at Diablo Ridge. He sat in the driver's seat of the Jeep where he was backed up against a large boulder where his back was out of sight from the trail. The black windbreaker he wore felt good, as the wind coming across the ridge was chilly. The jacket also covered the 9mm pistol resting in the holster on his right hip.

His steady eyes moved carefully over the terrain looking for any unusual movements coming from the ridge.

Off, in the distance, he heard the faint sound of what he thought was an ATV moving toward him. He listened as the noise got nearer, and then he spotted a fast-moving ATV weaving in and around boulders climbing up the trail. The rider was wearing all black, including a full-face black helmet with a tinted face shield.

"Damn, it's the Durango Kid," he said out loud. He laughed at his joke.

Dallas remained in the Jeep until the rider saw him and brought the machine to a sudden halt about ten feet away from the Jeep.

He saw that the rider was slender and not very large. Observing what the rider would do, Dallas was the first one to make a move. He slowly climbed out of the driver's seat keeping his eyes on the person who sat firmly on the ATV. He walked two more steps and stopped a few feet from the mysterious person.

"If you got something to tell me, then take that goddamn helmet off so I can see who I'm talking too."

With both hands, the rider reached up and slowly removed the helmet. Long, black hair fell down around the shoulders of Ivanna Mendoza. The beautiful features of her face caused Dallas to blink and take a closer look.

"Why you look surprised, Mr McCall," she said, a big grin on her face.

Dallas smiled, "Yes, I am surprised to see you, Mrs Mendoza."

She sat her helmet on the fuel tank and swung her long leg over the seat and within seconds, she was standing not two feet from Dallas. She stood very still for a moment her dark eyes exploring his face and then his eyes.

"No one knows that I am here, so we can speak freely. You need my help, and I need your help." Her voice was deep, clear and sexy.

"How's that going to work?"

Ivanna inched closer to Dallas. He could smell the fragrance of her perfume and deeply inhaled her woman scents. He could not help but notice she had unzipped the top of her leather-riding suit low enough to where her cleavage and the top of her breasts were visible to him. Her dark eyes and full moist lips weakened the tough former Marine. *Damn, I wonder if she is wearing anything under her skin-tight leathers.*

"You want revenge for the death of your friend Carlos; I can help you with that. I want revenge for the men who are trying to steal our homestead and drive us Mexican ranchers away so they can make millions of dollars tearing up our land. I hope that you can help me with my problem. Somehow, we can come up with a plan for us both to win."

Dallas studied her eyes and facial expressions while she talked. *I think she is sincere and means business.* "How is it that you have information about Carlos' murder?"

A mischievous smile crossed her lips; her dark eyes fixed on Dallas. "I'm not sure if you know much about the loyalty of Mexicans, or if Carlos told you how close our people are with each other. Well, I was told by a reliable source that he knew who hired the hitman to kill Carlos."

Why is she telling me this and not the sheriff? "If that is true and I find that person, then I will be indebted to you, and I will help you with whatever your problem is. Have you informed the sheriff about the murder for hire contract?"

"Thank you. I was informed in secrecy that Ty Denton hired a professional assassin to murder Carlos. I have no proof, only the word of the man who told me this. If you could make Ty talk and admit that he hired the killer, then the murderer could be found and brought to justice. No, I have not contacted the sheriff. I am the only person the man told about the contract. Now you know."

Dallas took in and let out a deep breath of air. "That's more than what I've been able to find out since I arrived. I am waiting for the right time to speak with Ty Denton. I will make it a point to look him up and get him to talk. Now, what is the problem you have that requires my assistance?"

She stood quietly and closed her eyes for a split second, and then fixed her eyes on Dallas. "It revolves around our land and the vultures that want to steal it from us. My husband thinks that because we own so much property and have money that we have no problems with people wanting to drive us away from our home. He is badly mistaken, in my opinion. The Garcia ranch is what the investors want, mainly because of the constant water level coming from the underground spring at their pond. The culprit behind this attempt to drive us away is Bill Denton and his son. So, we have our problem makers living in the same house. How convenient is that?" She tilted her head slightly to one side and smiled.

Dallas could not help but laugh at Ivanna's way of putting her words together. "I'd say that is mighty convenient. I can work both of our problems from the same family if what you tell me is true. The Denton's have plenty of hired hands who will protect them. I'll come up with a plan to get them away from their security blankets and speak to them."

"That is wonderful, Mr McCall."

"Please call me Dallas."

"Of course. My name is Ivanna."

Dallas smiled and extended his right hand to Ivanna. "Partners in crime?"

She took his hand and then moved to him, pressing her body against his and putting her arms around his neck and kissing him firmly on his lips. "Now, we are trusting partners sealed with a kiss. Let me have your cell phone." She moved away from him and held her hand out. "Your cell phone, please."

With a puzzled look on his face, he pulled the phone from his jacket pocket and handed it to her. She entered her cell phone number and saved it to his contacts. She returned the phone, smiled and walked to her ATV, straddled it, put on her helmet, cranked up the engine and waved at Dallas. She then sped off down the rocky path the same way she arrived.

Dallas stood and watched her until she was out of sight. *Now, that is a woman worth working with. To find out who murdered Carlos will close a sad chapter for the Garcia family and me. I hope she is telling me the truth. If so, I can go back to Texas and move on with my life.*

Dallas drove back to town, and for the first time since he had been coming to Diablo Ridge, he felt that he had accomplished something positive toward finding out who killed Carlos. At least he had names of possible suspects and people who are getting nervous, making threatening phone calls to him.

Lori walked briskly to meet Dallas as he pulled into the driveway of the garage. "Hey, cowboy. What have you been up to?"

He climbed out of the Jeep and faced the red-haired beauty. "Oh, still six feet three inches tall." He smiled. "Just riding around, looking for women who want to play around and have wild sex with a Texas cowboy."

She moved nearer to him and punched him playfully in the stomach. "You got more woman here than you can handle, cowboy."

He grunted, "I heard that. How about dinner tonight? I mean how about dinner at your house? There is only one place to eat in this one-horse town, and the M&J Café could use a new menu."

She giggled. "You're on. Come over early and stay late. Say, six o'clock, and I will grill steaks. Tonight is my grandparent's favourite TV night so they will stay in their little flat, and we will be all alone. How about that?"

"I like it. Especially the steak part. I can drop by the grocery and buy the steaks." He smiled and pulled his head back from her playful punch aimed at him.

"I already have prime-cut steaks. Come to think of it. Why don't we make that five o'clock? We can get some playtime in before dinner."

"Damn...I better get going and wash the New Mexico dirt off my body. See you later." He caught the kiss she blew to him, and he winked at her. He sped off up the street towards his empty room at the town's only bed and breakfast.

Sitting side by side at the dining room table, Dallas and Lori smiled and made eyes at each other as they ate dinner.

"You did a great job grilling these steaks," Dallas told Lori as he cut off another slice of the ribeye that covered over half of his plate.

"Thanks, they're pretty good, even if I do say so myself. I've had a lot of practice grilling as there is no man around except for grandpa, and he is not able to do what he loves to do anymore. He loves to cook outside, mainly on an open campfire. He calls that cowboy trail cooking."

"That is exactly what we call campfire cooking." Dallas took a sip of wine, sat the glass down on the table, turned his head to face Lori. "Do you know Ivanna Mendoza?"

She gave him a puzzled look. "Yes, I have met her on a few occasions. She is a gorgeous woman. Why do you ask?"

I can't tell her the truth just yet. "Oh, just wondering. I met her and her husband at the Garcia ranch last week. They seemed to me like really nice people. Carla told me they owned one of the largest ranches in the state."

"Yes, their ranch is large, and they are quite wealthy. They have a son, Diego, who is a little weird, so I've heard from the gossipers in town. I have never heard of him causing any trouble. Mr Mendoza keeps his hired hands from causing trouble. I've only seen them in town on a Saturday, and they seem to stick to themselves, drinking beer and playing guitars from the tailgates of their pickup trucks."

Dallas nodded and smiled. "What do you have in mind for us to do after dinner?"

She clasped her hands together, her elbows on the table and drew a long breath. "Grandma and Grandpa are busy. How about me showing you my bedroom?"

Dallas gave her a sharp look followed by a mischievous smile. "I like your idea."

Lori's bedroom came alive with their legs intertwined as one. The soft squeak of the bed, the deepness of their breath and the sound of their groans, and whispering love words to each other is the only thing that was heard in the quiet darkness of the room.

Wearing her white housecoat, Lori kissed her man and quietly let Dallas out of the front door a little after midnight.

He drove back to the B&B; a smile of happiness and content crossing his tanned face. In his mind, he could still remember how beautiful Lori looked, her shoulders completely covered with flocks of her red hair. *Damn, I must be in love with her. No, you can't feel that way, not now!*

Chapter 17

Monday, October 15

It was a sharp, crisp, typical early autumn morning when Dallas drove out of town toward the vast emptiness of the southwestern New Mexico's high desert grassland. The two-lane ranch road with open prairies on each side was deserted. He never met a single vehicle or saw a living thing until the prairie turned to green with pastureland as far as he could see and cattle roamed in vast herds along the floor of the valley.

Okay, so this must be the southern sector of the Denton ranch. The Garcia ranch is to the northeast. If the Denton's were to buy Romon's land, then they would have one or maybe the largest ranch in this part of the state. Romon and Carla said they would never think of selling the land for any amount of money. With Carlos out of the way, I believe the Denton's may be working with outside developers to persuade the Garcias to sell to them. With their constant water supply from the spring, there would always be water, which is the most valuable resource in this part of New Mexico. What an ideal location for hunting lodges or dude ranches. There is flat land in the valley that would accommodate a landing strip for a Gulfstream or a Learjet. I know Carlos must have been a thorn in their side, fighting to keep the land for cattle and not expensive resort ranches.

Coming toward him at a slow speed was a green pickup truck. As the Jeep and truck drew, nearer the truck came to a complete stop, and the driver held an arm outside the window.

Dallas pulled to a stop adjacent to the open window of the vehicle. An older Mexican man wearing a cowboy hat sat in the driver's seat, and a young boy wearing an Arizona Diamondbacks baseball cap sat in the passenger seat.

The man, grinning, said, "Howdy. You must be the stranger they call McCall?"

Dallas nodded and replied, "Howdy, yes, sir. I'm McCall."

"The name is Sergio Morales. This is my son, Pablo. I, along with my older son, own the ranch back down the road behind us. We heard how you are helping the Garcias find out who murdered their son, Carlos. For what it's worth, Bill Denton and his son are behind all the trouble being caused by wanting us smaller ranchers to see our land. It ain't gonna' happen. Let me know if I can be any help to you. You are welcome anytime at our ranch. My oldest son, Antonio, is at the ranch. If you want to talk with him, stop by. He was a friend of Carlos. Adios." He grinned again and drove away before Dallas could reply.

Dallas decided to accept the invitation since he was near the ranch. *I've heard Bill Denton's name since I arrived in Little Creek, and I have not met him yet; only his son Ty, but we have never had a private conversation. That is the sheriff's job to question him, not mine. I will make it my business to meet the Denton's, just as I have planned – and soon!*

The Morales ranch sat in a valley surrounded with green pastures and tall trees and was well-watered with a stock pond near the entrance road leading to the house and outbuildings.

A clump of cottonwoods surrounded a good-sized adobe house. He saw a corral and three cowboys sitting on the fence, watching another cowboy exercise a prancing horse. They all turned their heads to the Jeep as Dallas brought it to a halt twenty feet or so away.

One of the men jumped down from the fence and approached Dallas. He wore denim jeans and jacket, a slouchy sombrero on his head.

"Can I help you?" the cowboy asked coldly.

"The name is McCall. I met your father and brother along the road a few minutes ago and they told me you were friends with Carlos Garcia?"

The cowboy's dark eyes glared for an instant, and then a smile crossed his tanned face. He pulled off the leather glove from his right hand and extended it to Dallas. "You're the stranger in town and a Marine friend of Carlos?"

Dallas gripped his hand. "Yes, sir, that would be me."

"I am Antonio. Let's go to the house, it's about time for a coffee break."

Dallas readily agreed and walked to the side of the Mexican cowboy. Ahead of them, a pretty young woman watched them from the door of the house as they approached.

Antonio smiled and stopped in front of the woman. "Mr McCall, this is my wife, Victoria."

Her smile was broad and cheerful. "Welcome to our home. My friend, Carla Garcia, told me about you. Please come in. I have coffee and cake ready."

They were seated at a long table in a large and open typical Mexican decorated kitchen. The sweet smell of spices filled Dallas's nostrils just at it did at Rosa Garcia's kitchen.

"So, is there any news on who murdered Carlos?" Antonio asked.

Dallas shook his head. "Afraid not. The sheriff has not found enough clues even to question anyone who may be suspect. There are no eyewitnesses that we know of. I am not a lawman, so my hands are somewhat tied. But I plan on finding out who the coward or cowards were who ambushed him and left him dead on Diablo Ridge."

Antonio replied, "Us Mexican ranchers all know that Bill Denton is behind the investors wanting to buy us all out at low prices. What we cannot figure out is why Carlos was murdered or who would want to kill him! He stood up to Denton to protect his family ranch and that of his neighbors. He was our hero."

Dallas looked disgusted. "Carlos was my friend, and he always stood up for his fellow Marines. I've heard enough about the Dentons, and I aim to confront him and his son and ranch hand bullies. I have been in contact with the county sheriff, and his department is investigating."

Antonio said, "My family and other ranchers will help you, and we will back you, just let us know what we can do."

"Thanks, that means a lot to me." The two men shook hands and Dallas smiled at Victoria. "I liked your cake, and the coffee was strong, just as I like it – cowboy style. Thank you, ma'am."

As Dallas drove away from the ranch, he felt good about Antonio and the way he spoke his mind. *I like him and his wife. They are good people and are valuable Mexican-American ranchers to the state of New Mexico.*

His thoughts about what people have been telling him about the Denton's wanting to take over the Mexican owned ranch lands caused him to believe that Carlos' murder was linked to the Dentons.

Chapter 18

It was just after one o'clock when Dallas entered the county sheriff's office. For the first time since he had visited the sheriff, he saw two uniformed deputies sitting at desks.

The deputy nearest the door looked up at Dallas. "May I help you, sir?"

"Howdy. My name is McCall. Is the sheriff in?"

"Yes, sir. He's in his office. Go on back."

Dan Baker greeted Dallas as he rapped on the open doorway to the sheriff's office. "Come in. I've been hoping you would stop by."

"Yeah, I thought it was about time for us to have another conversation."

"I've been up since dawn, searching through piles of old department records." Papers covered his desk, and on a chair alongside the desk. He dragged another chair to the side of his desk. "Have a seat. Let me share with you something I found. This was a post from The Wall Street Journal earlier this year before I was elected sheriff."

Dan read out loud, "Billionaire execs are buying ranches for the cattle operations, game-hunting, and entertaining clients and guests near the small town of Little Creek, New Mexico. It was a showdown in New Mexico earlier this year, as two billionaires, one from Fort Worth, Texas, and one, cattle baron, Bill Denton from Little Creek battled it out to buy two large cattle ranches owned by Mexican-Americans in the Diablo Ridge area. Neither of the two ranch owners agreed to sell their homesteads."

Dallas grinned. "Now we are getting somewhere. What you have here is what I want to talk to you about. Do you agree with me that we need to have a long talk with Bill Denton?"

"Yes, I do agree with you, and that is what I plan to do. Since you are not a law enforcement official, you have no legal right to accompany me when I question Denton."

"I understand. The question I hope you ask him is: did you or your son, Ty, threatened to kill Carlos and burn down his family ranch? Carlos wrote this in his ledger on July 16. You have a copy of that entry in the investigation file."

"Yes, that will be a question I will ask him. If he denies that he threatened them, then he is lying as there were witnesses who heard the threat to Carlos – right? I will need to reread the remarks that Carlos wrote before I question the Denton's."

"No, Carlos did not mention if there were other people around that heard the threats. This may be a problem proving the Denton's made the threat," Dallas said in a sullen voice.

"I'll take one of my deputies with me, and we will drive out to the Denton ranch this afternoon. Have you dug up any clues as to who and why Carlos was murdered?"

"I have, maybe." He told Dan about his secret meeting with Ivanna Mendoza, and there was a contract on Carlos with a hitman being hired by Ty Denton. "We may find out she is not telling the truth, I hope not. I made a promise to Ivanna that our meeting would remain a secret. I hope you will honour my promise to her?"

"Yes, of course, this is confidential police information. That's interesting. It's starting to make sense that Carlos was ambushed by a professional killer. I'm sure you have ideas on how we can find out who authorised the assassination?"

"Yes, but I need to talk to Bill and Ty Denton after you speak with them. I want to see their reactions when I bring up what I know from Carlos' ledger. Since they don't know anything about me except that I've had harsh words with Ty, and I am looking for whoever murdered Carlos. I plan to ask them questions about buying land for those wealthy land developers in Texas. Maybe I can find out more if they can be persuaded that's why I'm in town and not just to avenge Carlos's murder."

Dan smiled. "Damn good plan, but by now, I'm sure most everyone knows why you are in Little Creek. If you can pull that off, then the townspeople may loosen up a little and start talking and believing you are not a secret agent or detective and just a friend helping friends."

Dallas stood up from his chair and looked at the piles of paperwork scattered over Dan's office. "Good luck with whatever else it is you're looking for. Oh, I received a threatening phone call yesterday from a private cell phone number. I'll keep you up on any further calls I may get." Dallas smiled and walked out of the office, raising a friendly hand to the two deputies working at their desks as he passed by them.

Dallas felt that he should check in on the Garcias' and find out how they are doing since he called Carla and asked her to be extra careful about strange visitors. He stopped by Lori's garage to top on the gas tank on the Jeep before starting out on the rough ride to the ranch.

"Hello there, cowboy Where are you off to today, looking for bad guys?" She said with a sly smile.

Dallas laughed. "I'm out looking for beautiful women who want to have dinner with me this evening."

"Look no further…I'm your dinner date. My house at seven o'clock sharp. Any questions?"

"No, ma'am." He smiled as he replaced the fuel nozzle on the pump. "Put that on my bill, will you, sweetheart?"

"You got it. Be careful out there. See you later." She blew him a kiss as he drove away.

The warm sun was directly over Dallas's head as he turned into the lane leading to the Garcia ranch. To his left, sweeping from a herd of cattle, he saw a leggy chestnut horse, and in the saddle, he could tell that it was Carla by her dark hair flowing out from her cowboy hat blowing in the wind just as the horse's tail.

When Dallas brought the Jeep to a halt in front of the house, Carla came walking, almost running, from the corral to meet him.

"Hello," she sang out in her cheery voice.

"Hello yourself. I just thought that I'd better check up on you and your family. How have you been doing?"

"Oh, we're doing alright, thanks for asking. We have not had any problems with visitors. We've missed you. What have you been up too?"

"Oh, about six feet three inches and growing." He laughed at his usual reply to the question. "You must be stretched pretty thin taking care of all those cattle by yourself?"

With a slow, good-humoured smile, she said, "I'm doing just fine. Christian helps me when he is not in school. You want a job, cowboy?"

Dallas could not help but laugh out loud. "I might just take you up on that offer."

"How about some lunch? Mom and Dad are at the Mendoza ranch attending a church luncheon and Christian is at school."

"Just in time for lunch again," Dallas said smiling.

They walked to the back door and into the kitchen.

"There's beer in the fridge, you want to grab us a couple while I wash the dust off of me?"

A few minutes later, Dallas looked up when Carla returned to the kitchen. She had removed her chaps and changed her shirt for a white T-shirt that revealed her well-proportioned breasts. Her skin-tight jeans leave no doubt about her being a full-grown woman. *My lord, she is beautiful.*

"How about a roast beef sandwich?" Carla asked.

"That sounds good to me." Dallas watched her backside as she worked on preparing the lunch. *What a body that woman has. Tend to business, McCall.*

"Have you found out any more about who killed my brother?" She asked.

"I, along with the sheriff, have a few good leads, but no suspects. I've met a few of your neighbours who provided me with valuable information. The Morales family told me they were friends of yours, and they knew Carlos very well."

"Yes, they are good people. We have been friends for years." She sat the sandwich along with tortilla chips in front of him where he sat at the kitchen table. "Can I get you anything else?"

"No, thanks. This looks great. I wasn't looking for a meal; just wanting to see how you were doing."

Carla gave him a sharp glance. "I've heard you have been seeing a lot of Lori Porter lately. Is that right?"

He grinned. "Gossip travels fast in a small community. Now, who would spread such a rumour?"

"I have friends in town," she said… Her dark eyes were flashing.

"Yes, Carla. I have had dinner and lunch with Lori on a few occasions. I thought she was your friend?"

"She is my friend. I was just curious. Lori is a good woman." Carla turned her head and took a bite from her sandwich.

I think that she is jealous. Damn, she is only nineteen years old but a grown woman. I like her, and I love to look at her. She is gorgeous. I can't afford to get involved with the sister of my dead friend. I need to change the subject. "How has your dad been feeling?"

Carla gave Dallas a strange look and said, "He is doing very well, thanks for asking."

They both burst into laughter.

"I'm trying to seduce you, and you ask me how my father is doing." She covered her mouth with her hand in an attempt to control the laughter coming out of her mouth.

Dallas stopped laughing and looked calmly at her. "Do you think Carlos would approve of you wanting to go to bed with his best friend?"

She seemed astonished. "I don't understand you. I think Carlos would approve. After all, he introduced you to me a long time ago in our letters. Besides, I'm not a little sister…I'm a grown woman and can make my own choice of the man I want."

"Yes, he did, and I always looked forward to seeing your pictures. You are such a beautiful young woman, and you have your whole life ahead of you. Carlos was like a brother to me, and I would never do anything that would bring shame to his name. I am too old for you, and my future is not known. I am a one-woman man, believe that or not. I respect Lori and would do nothing to hurt her. I hope you understand what I'm telling you?"

Carla dropped her head and began to cry. "I do…I do understand, but it doesn't help much when I know in my heart that I am in love with you."

Dallas brought her to him and held her close. "I am honoured that you feel that way. Know that if it were under different circumstances, I would be all over you. Now, dry those eyes and walk me out to the Jeep. You have cows that are missing you."

She slapped him on the arm and said between sobs, "Cows, my ass. You better get to moving, or I might change my mind and get my father's shotgun after you and force you to come with me to my bedroom."

Dallas kissed her on the forehead and wiped the tears from her eyes with the back of his hand. "See you later, sweet woman.

Thanks for lunch." He let go of her and walked out of the house to where his Jeep was parked.

As he drove away, Carla looked out of the kitchen window, tears continued to flow down her cheeks. "See you later, cowboy," she whispered out loud.

"Call me if you have any trouble." *Damn, McCall, how and why did you turn down that beautiful woman's offer to make love to her. Stupid or faithful! My guess is – more stupid then faithful. Hell, I'm not engaged or married to Lori.*

Dinner that evening with Lori was filled with laughter and happiness as Dallas felt the bonding and trust between them. *I'm falling for this beautiful woman, and I have the feeling that she likes me more than a friend. And I was near to having sex with another woman a few hours ago, and here I am with a woman that I don't deserve. You're an asshole, McCall.*

On his way back to his room, he saw headlights flicker in the side mirror of the Jeep. He never paid much attention to the vehicle behind him until he pulled into the parking area of the B&B, and the car behind him turned in and stopped. Dallas jumped out of the Jeep and walked rapidly back to the car sitting with the lights on and the engine running. When Dallas stopped at the driver's side of the vehicle, he saw the smiling face of Sheriff Dan Baker.

"Good evening, stranger. Are you out for a late evening joy ride?"

Dallas laughed. "Looking for drunk drivers to help pay your electric bill, are you?"

"No, just making my nightly rounds and saw you leaving Lori Porter's house. She is a nice woman. She and my wife are good friends."

"Yes, her and her grandparents are very nice people. Do you need me for anything besides harassing me?"

Dan laughed. "No. You're not on my most wanted list. Enjoy your evening. Drop by for a cup of coffee when you find the time."

"Roger that."

After preparing for bed, Dallas received a text message from Ivanna. *Meet me tomorrow morning on Diablo Ridge at 10:30. Sleep tight.*

What in the hell does that woman want now? I will find out tomorrow morning.

Chapter 19

Tuesday Morning, October 22

The sun rose and warmed the chill air as Dallas drove towards Diablo Ridge where Ivanna asked him to meet her. *I hope she has come across with more information that will help me go after whoever killed Carlos.*

It was ten-thirty-five when Ivanna pulled the ATV to a sliding halt near to where Dallas stood next to the Jeep. Dressed in her tight black leathers, she removed her helmet and swung her leg off of the ATV and approached Dallas.

"Hey, Texas man. How have you been doing?" Her radiant smile lit up her gorgeous face.

"Hanging in there. How's the detective business going?"

She laughed softly. "I don't believe that I want to be a full-time crime investigator. I feel more like a…like a snitch."

Dallas laughed at her remarks. "I share your feelings except for the snitch part. We are trying to find out who and why my friend was murdered, and who is the real financer behind the bid to buy out all of the local ranchers, including your family ranch. I call that crime work."

"Yes, and I am sad to tell you that the person who told me in secrecy that Ty Denton hired the hitman that killed Carlos is my son, Diego. Why Ty told him what he did, I don't know, but I fear for my son." She stood tall and firm, tears formed in her eyes.

"Damn. If Diego knew this, then he may not be involved with any wrongdoings; just one of his friend's blowing of bull crap to another friend."

Ivanna raised her head, and through her moist eyes, she looked at Dallas. "Oh, God, I hope Diego is not involved. He is a troubled boy, but he has a good heart and knows right from wrong. His father would die if he knew our son was mixed up with Ty." She dropped her head again.

"Ivanna," At his voice, she looked up and gracefully tossed her long hair over her shoulder, "It is now the time for me to have that talk with Ty Denton. No more waiting around for answers he or his father gives to the sheriff. I will take care of it – I promise you that."

She gracefully moved to him, placing her arms around his neck, pressing her body firmly to his and kissing his lips. She pulled her head back; her body remained hard against his, and her arms were warm on his neck. Their eyes met.

"Thank you. I have so much respect and feelings for you...I am really attracted to you," she said in a near whisper.

"You have a nice way of thanking me." Dallas gently pulled her arms down from his neck and held her hands. "Another time, another place, pretty lady. You had better get back to your ranch before you are missed. I will keep you abreast of what happens. Be safe." He left her standing alone, jumped into the Jeep and drove away.

Damn, why am I so lucky? Two women I could take to bed, and I turned them both down. Lori is too special to me, and I will not cheat on her. She is a woman that I can trust and count on to brighten my day. Now, my plan to deal with Ty Denton.

After returning to Little Creek, Dallas dropped by the sheriff's office and talked with him about how his visit to the Denton ranch went.

Dan said, "I never found out anything that we didn't know. Bill Denton admitted that he was working with potential out of state investors trying to buy local ranches. There is no crime in what he is doing. His son, Ty, was not at the ranch, and Bill told me his son was not involved with the investors, and he also stated that he nor Ty ever threatened Carlos."

Dallas turned his body in the chair. "Well, we both know that is a crock of shit. You don't know this, but I'm going to have a long chat with Ty Denton. He may file charges against me when I'm finished, but I will deny that I did anything wrong."

"Don't do anything foolish that is against the law. We have too good of a relationship and understanding for it to end by me arresting you."

Dallas gave Dan a stern look. "This has gone on long enough. I want Carlos' killers brought to justice with or without the support of the law. I value our friendship, but my loyalty lies with my dead friend and his family. I'll keep you informed of what I am doing. Adios." He rose from his chair and walked out of the office with a slight limp.

Dark clouds rolled in and blacked out the afternoon sun as Dallas drove the Jeep toward the Denton ranch. About halfway from town, Dallas saw a white pickup coming toward him on the opposite side of the ranch road. As the truck passed by, Dallas saw the driver was Ty Denton.

Dallas slowed the Jeep down and made a quick U-turn and chased after the truck. *I can never catch him if he identifies me, but I can keep the pickup truck in view and follow him until he stops. He surely knows by now I drive Lori's rental Jeep.*

As Dallas drew nearer behind the truck, he made out the image of a person sitting in the passenger seat. *Yep, it's the little wimp, Weasel. I bet he sleeps in that beat-up black cowboy hat.*

Rounding a sharp curve, Dallas saw the truck accelerated and was speeding away from him. *Ty spotted me. He knows that it's me driving the Jeep. There is no reason for me trying to keep up with him and kill myself. I can easily find the vehicle. He must know that I am after him and want some answers about Carlos's murder.*

Going around another curve, Dallas saw Ty's pickup parked crossways in the road. He slammed on the brakes sliding to a sudden stop. In front of him stood Ty and Weasel both holding rifles pointed at him.

Dallas raised up and loosened his pistol from the waistband holster on his jeans and sat waiting for someone to speak.

"Out of the Jeep," Ty ordered. "Now, get out and walk slowly over here."

Baby boy has got some guts. I doubt if either one of them has shot anything except wild game. Dallas slowly climbed out of the Jeep and stopped in front of the two-armed cowboys and grinned. "If you boys want to talk with me, you won't need those rifles."

Ty appeared nervous when he said, "Why are you following us?"

"Who says that I'm following you? It's a public road, and I am going to town. Is that a reason to pull guns on me?"

"Who the hell are you anyway?" Ty asked. "You have been dogging me for the past few weeks. What do you want with me?"

Dallas slowly moved toward the two keeping his eyes on the trigger fingers that held the rifles. "You know that I am a friend of Carlos Garcia, and I think you know who killed him."

Ty stiffened, and his jaws tightened. "I don't know anything about who murdered Carlos. My father is Bill Denton, and he will have your hide for harassing me. He will…"

Dallas raised his voice. "Shut your goddamn mouth, boy. I know who your father is, and he will not bother me in the least." Dallas took a quick step forward and ripped the rifle out of Ty's hands. A shot rang out, and a bullet from Weasel's rifle grazed Dallas' left arm. Dallas quickly stepped to where Weasel stood with his mouth open and jerked the gun away from him and struck him upside the head with the butt of the rifle. Weasel screamed as the blood ran down the side of his face.

Dallas turned to Ty, who stood like a stone statue; his face was white, and his eyes bugged out from fright.

Dallas said to Weasel, "You, tough guy with the blood all over you, get your ass over here and stand next to your spineless friend."

Weasel stammered, "Don't hit me again. I need a doctor."

"You will need an undertaker if you ever pull a weapon on me again." Dallas raised his arm and wiped the blood from his wounded arm across Weasel's face.

Dallas grabbed hold of Weasel's shirt collar and pulled him against the side of the pickup. He then took hold of Ty's arm and threw him to the pavement. Dallas pulled the pistol from his waistband and held it against Ty's forehead.

"I have nothing to lose by blowing your head off. The only witness is your buddy here who will be dead along with you. Now, tell me who killed Carlos Garcia?"

Ty began to whimper, and his body trembled. "I don't know, please, trust me, I had nothing to do with his death, please don't kill me, I don't want to die."

"You're lying. I'll give you five seconds to tell me who killed my friend or I will blow your brains out."

"Okay…okay, don't kill me. I only know that a man from Sant Fe was paid to kill Carlos. That is all I know, I swear."

"Not good enough. Who hired the hitman and what is his name?" Dallas applied more pressure with the pistol to Ty's forehead. "It's your last chance. Tell me the name of the man who killed Carlos."

"He will kill me if I tell you his name."

Dallas laughed. "You are super stupid. I will kill if you don't tell me. You must have been absent from the college class that taught stupidity. Oh, to hell with it. I'm sick of screwing with you. Say goodbye to your friend over there who is pissing in his pants."

"No, no, don't shoot. I will tell you his name. He is...his name is Delbert Norton. That's all I know. Please, you've got to believe me."

"Why in the hell should I believe you? I think that you hired him to get rid of Carlos so your daddy could buy out the Garcia ranch. Isn't that so?"

"No, I only heard his name from one of our ranch hands. Someone hired the hitman and tried to blame me. I didn't do it. Please let me go."

Dallas pulled the pistol barrel away from Ty's head and jerked him to his feet. "Now get your ass out of here and take your tough friend with the wet jeans along with you. If I hear that you filed a complaint against me with the sheriff, I will hunt you down and kill you before he can arrest me."

Ty and Weasel staggered to the truck and climbed in. He started the engine, turned the pickup around and drove back the way they came from.

Dallas climbed into the Jeep and rolled up his shirtsleeve on his left arm and inspected the wound. *Nothing serious, just a gash.* He tied his handkerchief around the wound. *Ty must be running home to daddy. I hope he scares the shit out of his old man. Now, to hunt down Delbert Norton. When I find him, I will get the answer as to who hired him to kill Carlos.*

Dallas treated his wound in his room, changed shirts and jacket and made a quick stop at the sheriff's office to inform Dan about what happened.

"Sounds like a good case of, 'Stand Your Ground' to me," Dan said. "I could arrest them if you want to press charges."

Dallas grinned. "That's what it was! No, I don't want to press charges. I want them to know that I am not afraid of them. Would you find out through your police network who Delbert Norton is? I would appreciate knowing more about him before asking you to arrest him."

"This is police work, Dallas. I suggest that you step back and let us do our job."

"Sheriff, you involved me when we agreed to you sharing information on the case with me. I will not lay low until Carlos' killer and the person who hired him is brought to justice. And, that my friend is your job."

Dan shook his head in slow, decisive motion. "You're getting too deep, my friend. Just be careful whatever you plan to do."

"I'm always careful. That's how I've survived to live for twenty-eight years and three years in combat." Dallas nodded and walked out of the office.

Later that day, a couple of hours before sunset, Dallas treated his wound again at his room. *That bullet could have killed me. I lucked out again.*

He ate a supper consisting of a cold meat sandwich, dill pickles and two beers. He doubled up on pain pills and fell asleep fully clothed on the bed.

Dallas woke up at six-thirty, his arm throbbing. Two more pain pills and he went downstairs for breakfast.

Mrs Norris filled his coffee cup and sat a plate filled with a short stack of buttermilk pancakes, three pieces of bacon along with a pitcher of hot syrup in front of him along with a copy of the Santa Fe newspaper.

She smiled at Dallas and said cheerfully, "You have a nice day, Mr McCall."

"Thanks, Mrs Norris. You have a good day yourself." *I guess she is getting accustomed to the stranger in town staying at her boarding house.*

Chapter 20

It was around nine o'clock, when Dallas drove down the main street of town on his way to see Lori at her garage. As he rode along the mainly deserted street, he thought about Ty, Weasel and John Badger. *They're all a bunch of cowards. As long as you aren't afraid of them, none of them wants to start anything.*

He pulled into the driveway and stopped at the gas pump. From the garage office came the graceful figure of Lori wearing tight-fitting jeans and a black sweatshirt. Her glossy red hair gathered into a ponytail bounced off her back.

"Hey, cowboy. Where have you been hiding?"

Dallas smiled and turned to meet her. "Oh, just roaming around causing trouble. How have you been doing?"

Lori laughed. Her green eyes resting upon Dallas glowed brightly. She replied in her warm, cheerful voice, "I've been working and waiting for you to come by to see me. I missed you."

"I've missed you too. How about you invite me to dinner this evening?"

She laughed, "You are a bold son of a gun, but I love it. You bet. What are you hungry for?"

"Oh, how about a tall, beautiful red-headed woman with ruby read lips and a smile to die for?"

She gave him a coy smile. "You already have that, cowboy. Now, what would you like for me to cook for dinner?"

"Can you fix chicken fried steak with milk gravy?"

"Of course, I can. I'll do mashed potatoes and pinto beans and cornbread. How does that sound?"

"Oh, lord woman. I don't deserve you. That will be great. Sorry for my bad manners asking you if you would prepare a meal for me."

"I love cooking for you. If the truth is to be known, I'm in love with you." Her face turned red, and she put a hand to her mouth. "Oops!"

Dallas smiled and moved to her and took her in his arms. They embraced next to the gas pump. Dallas did not reply to her remarks. *Oh, no. I can't afford for her to love me – not now!*

They smiled at each other as they stood in the open driveway, the smell of gasoline filling the air around them.

"See you at seven," Lori said.

"Great. What was it I came here for?" They laughed as their eyes danced with joy.

Dallas stopped at the Telegraph office where he had picked up his box that held his pistol and personal items. He saw the sign, 'Use our computer no charge' hanging on the wall.

"Can I use your computer?" Dallas asked the old man sitting in a swivel chair at a desk behind the counter.

The man looked up and took another look at Dallas. "Oh, yes, sir. Help yourself, Mr McCall."

Dallas sat down in front of the desktop computer, used the generic password taped to the bottom of the screen. He located the google screen and typed Delbert Norton. He found he had a website advertising himself as a private security contractor with his office located in Santa Fe. Dallas wrote down the telephone number and address. He read a couple of the reviews submitted supposedly by customers. Dallas knew after reading a few of the customer reviews that they were not written by actual customers.

After collecting the information he needed, Dallas thanked the old man and returned to his parked Jeep. *I have a plan. I will contact this man and request his assistance with a security problem I am having. I will meet him outside of town, kidnap him and take him to Diablo Ridge and force him to confess that he killed Carlos and who hired him to do so. A piece of cake.* Dallas laughed to himself at his kidnap plan.

Dallas made the telephone call to the man with the name, Delbert Norton. He agreed to meet Dallas on Friday outside of Little Creek. An upfront retainer fee of five hundred dollars cash was promised to be paid by Dallas when they met. *My plan should work. After I'm finished with the man, and if he is the killer, then I will turn him over to the sheriff. I might work him over a little just for the hell of it before delivering him to Dan.*

At six o'clock, Lori was waiting for Dallas on the porch of her house. When he met her, she embraced him and kissed him repeatedly on the lips, face and neck. "Oh, I am so happy to see you."

"Me too. It's only been a couple of hours since we were together. I like the greeting."

"I know, and I don't care. Now that we have let our true feelings out for each other, we can just love and enjoy each other."

"Amen to that."

She took him by the hand and led him to the kitchen. "I have margaritas mixed for us before we have dinner."

"That sounds good to me. I smell steak frying?"

"You sure do, and lots of it. Grab a stool there at the counter."

They sat side by side sipping on their Mexican Kool-Aid.

Lori moved her hand to Dallas's leg, then she began rubbing his thigh her eyes flashed, a sudden strong emotion. "You're looking mighty handsome tonight, cowboy."

"Thanks. You are as gorgeous as always and the most beautiful woman I have ever seen." They leaned in toward each other, and their lips met. The sound of the timer buzzing broke up their kiss.

"The cornbread is done. You ready to eat?"

"I'm always ready to eat."

"Damn, Lori. This meat is so tender I can cut it with a fork. You did a great job on the gravy. I love gravy to cover a big pile of mashed potatoes. The pintos and cornbread are so good. I would get fat if I ate this way every day."

"You could use a little more meat on your muscled body. I'll keep you trimmed down with lots and lots of making love."

Dallas smiled, "I heard that."

After dinner, Lori took Dallas back to say hello to her grandparents. "They always ask about you," Lori said. "They like you and so do I."

Later in the evening after making love, they laid in each other's arms in Lori's queen-size bed. She put her cheek on Dallas's chest and ran her fingers over and around his stomach. Lori felt safe and protected when she was with her cowboy.

It was near midnight when Dallas arrived back to his room. Sleep came quickly as his stomach was full and his sexual appetite was fully satisfied.

The following morning, Dallas made a practice run to Diablo Ridge and walked around the rocks where he thought the killer must have fired the first shots at Carlos. Tomorrow, with luck, he would bring Delbert Norton here handcuffed and threaten him with his life if he didn't tell him what he wanted to know. *He must be a cheap hitman to advertise on the Internet. From what I've heard, the pros have a go-between person to introduce them to clients. He may kill me before I take him down. Oh, well. It's worth the risk for Carlos' revenge.*

Upon the return drive to town, he parked the Jeep at a turn off from the ranch road three miles west of Little Creek. *This is where I told Norton to meet me at one o'clock Friday. Looks like the meeting location is safe as there are very few vehicles travelling on the road in the afternoon on a Friday.*

Friday near one o'clock, Dallas sat in the Jeep parked along the spot Delbert Norton agreed to meet him. The sun was bright, and there was a crisp breeze blowing in from the mountains. *A perfect day for a kidnapping.* He laughed softly out loud.

The sound of a car coming up the road caused Dallas to glance in the side mirror. A black Cadillac Escalade pulled in behind the Jeep and stopped. Dallas adjusted his pistol in his waistband and then climbed out of the driver's seat. Not really knowing what to expect, he walked slowly back to the SUV and stopped at the driver's side that had tinted windows.

The window slowly rolled down enough that Dallas saw a dark-complected man with a full black beard and long black hair sitting in the driver's seat. The man, who wore sunglasses, asked in a gruff voice, "You McCall?"

"Yep, I'm McCall. Are you Norton?"

Dallas quickly surveyed the inside of the vehicle looking for any hidden passengers. Norton was the only person in the car.

"You got the five hundred dollar retainer fee?" Norton asked.

Dallas nodded and reached into his jacket pocket and pulled out a letter-sized white envelope and handed it to the outreached hand of Norton through the open window. The man opened the envelope and ran his hand over the five one hundred dollar bills.

"Okay, tell me what you want?"

Dallas hesitated playing the same game as Norton. "I need for you to persuade a man that I want a loan repaid."

Norton turned his head and looked at Dallas. "How much is the loan?"

"Fifty grand," Dallas said, keeping a straight face with the lie he told.

"I get twenty percent if I collect the loan. If I don't, you owe me another five hundred."

Dallas nodded. "If the man doesn't pay the loan, I want him eliminated. Can you do that?"

Norton hesitated, "It will cost you if I were to do such a thing, not saying I would."

"How much would it cost me to get rid of him?"

"It depends on where the location is. You're looking at 60 to 100k. Do you have that kind of money?"

"Yeah, I have the money. I will take you to where he lives. It is a rough rocky road, and we will need to take my Jeep."

"How long will it take to show me the location?"

"Thirty, thirty-five minutes at the most."

Norton sat quietly without speaking moving his head around scanning the area. He rolled the window up and opened the door and climbed out of the driver's seat and hit a remote locking the doors.

Dallas now saw the man standing near him and sized him up. Norton was not a large man, maybe five feet six or seven and a slender build. He wore a black suit with a white shirt with an open collar. He faced Dallas and pulled back the left side of his jacket exposing a handgun resting in a shoulder holster.

You had better act fast, McCall. This guy looks dangerous.
Dallas walked toward the Jeep. Norton looked around again and then followed Dallas and climbed into the passenger seat.

"I hate these goddamn rough riding piece of shit off the road vehicles. Why would anyone want to live in this part of the country?" Norton spurted out.

"It's a way of life in this part of the country." Norton glanced to his right, which gave Dallas enough time to swiftly pull his pistol and stick the barrel in Norton's ribs. He slammed on the brakes, and the Jeep slid to a stop near the rocky edge of the road.

"I'll take that handgun." Dallas reached in and pulled out a .45 caliber semiautomatic Colt pistol from the shoulder holster. He then removed the envelope with the money from the other inside pocket. Dallas gave the Colt a toss into the weeds and rocks alongside the road and stuck the money envelope in the inside pocket of his jacket.

"You bastard, I will kill you," Norton yelled.

"I don't think so." Dallas hit him upside the head with the barrel of his pistol. He grabbed his arms and pulled them behind his back and slapped a pair of handcuffs on his wrists.

Blood ran down the side of Norton's face, and he tried to step out of the Jeep.

Dallas reached behind the seat where Norton sat and lifted up a coil of rope. Tying him to the Jeep seat, Dallas tapped him again on the head with his pistol. "Now, sit there and don't move, or I'll kick your ass down the side of the mountain and let the wild animals have you for supper."

Norton yelled out, "What the hell are you doing? What do you want from me anyway? I will kill you…bastard."

"Shut your damn mouth. You killed my friend, and we are going to the location where you ambushed and killed him like a wild animal while he lay wounded by your first shots."

"I don't know what you're talking about. I have never been anywhere near this shit hole of a place. You got me mixed up with someone else. Now, untie me and take these damn handcuffs off and take me back to my vehicle and I will forget this ever happened."

Dallas glared and him and continued driving. *What if he is telling the truth? I'll know more when I see his reactions when we arrive at Diablo Ridge.*

Dallas pulled the Jeep to a stop near the spot where Carlos was found. He untied the rope from around the passenger seat where Norton was sitting and tied the rope to his handcuffed wrists behind his back.

"Tell me about how you walked up to my friend who was lying here propped up against his ATV wounded from the bullets you put in him from up there on the ridge." Dallas pointed to where he thought the assassin's gunfire came from.

"You're crazy, I've never been here before, and I never killed the friend you are talking about. I never even heard his name before."

Dallas jerked on the rope and spun Norton around to face him. "You were hired to murder Carlos Garcia by rancher Ty Denton, isn't that right?"

Norton stood rigid. "Denton, that little bastard tried to hire me to kill a man, but I had no interest in murdering anyone. Hell, I am a debt collector, not an assassin. You gotta' believe me, mister. I have never been here or near this area in my life."

"What if I get you and Denton together and see who is lying. What do you think about that?"

"I wouldn't know him if I saw him. We only talked over our cell phones. He found my ad on the Internet. I use the word's hit man to get business. I could never kill anyone unless I were forced to. Hell, take me back to my SUV, keep the five hundred bucks and let me get out of this godforsaken place."

Dallas watched Norton's facial expressions and body language while he said about himself that he did not want other people to know. "Norton, I actually believe you. I don't approve of what you do for a living, but a man has got to live. I will let you go if I have your word that you will testify in court what you told me about Ty Denton."

"Yeah, hell yes. I will tell the judge everything."

Dallas removed the rope from Norton's wrists. "The cuffs stay on until I am sure you're telling me the truth. If I decide that you are lying to me, it will not bother me in the least to kill you."

By the time they returned to Norton's vehicle, Dallas was pretty much convinced that he did not murder Carlos. His testimony, even with his reputation, would be beneficial if Ty Denton was brought to trial. *Now, who killed Carlos and who hired him? Or, maybe no one was hired. I've still got a killer to catch.*

Dallas removed the handcuffs from Norton's wrists and gave the envelope with the five hundred dollars to him. "You deserve the money to buy another Colt .45. I'll see you in court."

Norton, a sly smile across his rugged face, unlocked the car alarm, climbed into the Cadillac, started the engine and turned around and sped off back towards the main highway outside of Little Creek.

Dallas jumped in the Jeep and followed the Cadillac to the junction of the highway leading to Santa Fe. When the vehicle was out of site, Dallas drove to the B&B guest parking area.

Dallas returned to his room and flopped down in the recliner near the window with a bottle of beer in his hand. *Damn, kinda back to day one. I still believe Ty Denton had something to do with Carlos' murder. He is a coward, I know that for sure. Badger and Weasel are phony tough guys and don't they have the nerve to shoot anyone. More detective work tomorrow.*

Chapter 21

Thursday, October 25
Little Creek

Dallas entered the small B&B dining room at six-thirty and sat at his usual two-chair table by the double window that overlooked the main street of town. Mrs Norris poured his coffee and laid a newspaper in front of him. "I have biscuits and sausage gravy this morning," she said with a charming smile.

"That sounds great, thanks."

There were three men, dressed in western attire sitting at a four-chair table next to the entrance to the dining room. Dallas could overhear their conversation, as their voices carried in the small dining room.

The older looking man of the three said, "I'm meeting with Bill Denton as his ranch later this morning. He told me on the phone that he had an update about his meeting with a Texas company that he met with recently. I may still have a chance to get my foot in the door when his plans are confirmed."

Dallas ate his breakfast and appeared to be reading the newspaper as not to let on that he heard every word the men said during their morning conversation. *The more I hear about Bill Denton, the more I dislike him. He may be an honest businessman, but he also is a greedy SOB. Sounds to me like the Garcia and the Morals ranches are the prime targets.*

After breakfast, Dallas drove to the parking area in front of the sheriff's office and parked the Jeep.

When he entered the office, Dan Baker was sitting alone in his office.

Dallas sat down in the lone chair in front of Dan's desk.

"You're up and around early as you always are," Dan said. "What have you been up to lately?"

Dallas gave Dan a detailed account of what happened between him and Norton.

"I have interrogated many enemy prisoners, and I believe that Norton was contacted by Ty Denton asking him to kill Carlos. Norton is not a real hitman. Hell, he would probably shoot his dick off in the processes of pulling the big .45 pistol he carries in a shoulder holster." He told Dan about the conversation he overheard between out of town businessmen during breakfast at the B&B this morning.

Dan was still smiling about Dallas's observation of Norton when he said, "I hear you. I could bring Denton in and lock him up for attempting to hire a person to commit murder, but his old man and their fancy lawyer would have him out of jail in no time. We know for a fact that Bill Denton and his son wants to buy out as many ranchers as he can. He's not doing anything illegal – so far!"

"Yes, I agree with you. How about me continuing to watch Ty Denton and see where all he goes and who he talks to. I would be less conspicuous than you or one of your deputies. I also want to keep an eye on Bill Denton and his whereabouts."

"Yes, you are right. I won't tell you what to do because it wouldn't do any good. Keep in mind that you are not acting in an official capacity as a deputy sheriff or police officer. You can make a citizen's arrest if you come across a situation that he should be arrested. Be careful around Bill Denton and his son. Since you know Ty Denton attempted to put a hit contract out on Carlos, he is capable of doing the same thing against you."

Dallas gave Dan a sharp look and then smiled sarcastically. "Yes, sir, sheriff. I hear you loud and clear."

Dan grinned, "When this is all over, how about us getting together and get rip-roaring drunk and talk about our service in the Marines?"

"Roger that. See you later." Dallas jumped up from the chair, and with a slight limp, left the office.

As Dallas drove toward Lori's garage to gas up the Jeep, he spotted Ty's pickup in front of the M&J café. *Think I'll grab a cup of coffee.* He swung the Jeep into a parking spot next to Ty's truck.

When Dallas entered the café, he saw Ty, Weasel and John Badger sitting at their usual corner table. Dallas gave a quick glance at them and proceeded to a stool at the counter, his back turned to the three friends. *They're too cowardly to walk up behind me, or even talk to me. I'll just make 'em squirm a little.* He smiled to himself.

Dallas finished his coffee and laid a dollar bill on the counter. *I'm gonna make them piss in their boots.* He turned from the stool, and as he neared the front entrance, he stopped, turned to face the men sitting at the corner table.

"Denton, I saw your friend from Santa Fe, Delbert Norton yesterday. He said to call him if you still wanted him to get rid of your friend. I think he said, the name was John Badger!"

Dallas laughed and walked out of the café and was still laughing when he drove the Jeep to the garage. *Damn, I would have liked to have stayed and seen what when on after I left.*

"Hey, pretty lady," Dallas said with a smile, as Lori met him at their usual meeting point – a gas pump. "How are you doing this fine morning?"

"I'm fine, thank you. You're mighty cheerful this morning. You haven't been out with other woman, have you?"

"No, not today. I was with a hot woman last night. I just feel like…smiling."

"I can make you smile more if you have time to join us for a meal at my house. Grandma is preparing a pot of chicken and dumplings, and she wants you to join us."

"Chicken and dumplings, one of my favorite meals. I would be honored. What time?"

"When she cooks a noon meal, she calls it dinner, and it is always served at noon. And, if it is an evening meal, then she calls it supper, and it is served at five o'clock sharp."

"This will be the first meal I've had with you three. I may not be finished with what I'm doing by noon. Can we make it at six for supper? I always like being with you, and I'm looking forward to getting to know your grandparents a little better. See you later, sweetheart. Got some business to do in the ranchlands."

Lori waved as Dallas drove off to the west. *I love that man so much. I only hope he has the time for me to get to know him better. I think he might be in love with me! He is still a stranger in town on a mission. I know he will succeed in finding out who killed his friend, Carlos.*

Dallas decided to drive out unannounced to the Morales ranch and talk with the owner's son, Antonio and his wife who he met last week. *I like them both and trust them, even though I only met them once. They are honest people.*

As he drove along the lonely stretch of the ranch road leading to the Morales ranch, he turned on the radio for the first time since renting the Jeep. When he flipped through the channels, all he heard was static before the sound of a man's voice announcing a welcome to the Public Radio station came blasting through the single speaker mounted under the dashboard. The announcer went on to say, "We're coming to you live from the Southwestern New Mexico town of, Marysville. This program is sponsored by the Bill Denton ranch outside of Little Creek." Dallas turned up the volume, then the station faded out.

Old man Denton got his hands in everything around the county and the whole state. He sure has the money to hire a contract killer, and his son surely has access to the finances. Maybe Bill Denton was the one who hired a hitman to kill Carlos? I've got to figure out a way to expose Denton as a suspect in the murder.

Antonio was working on the engine of a farm tractor along with a ranch hand when Dallas arrived at the ranch. He drove near the men and parked the Jeep. He walked stiffly toward them.

"Troubles?" Dallas said, as he stopped beside Antonio.

"There is always something to repair on a ranch. How are you, my friend?" Antonio asked, as he turned to Dallas. "Excuse me for not shaking your hand." He held up a greasy right hand and smiled.

"No problem. I was in the area, so I thought I'd stop by and say howdy."

Antonio spoke to the man working with him in Spanish and patted him on the back. He turned to Dallas, "Come on up to the house, and I will wash up. I know Victoria will have a fresh pot of coffee on the stove and some cookies."

Dallas greeted the smiling Victoria at the kitchen door. "Come in please, Mr McCall," she said with a welcome smile.

Antonio and Dallas sat at the kitchen table, as Victoria sat down a plate of chocolate cookies and a pot of coffee and cups in front of them.

"We had visitors yesterday," Antonio said. "Bill Denton, his son, Ty and a man from Texas who was introduced as an agent for a land development company in Houston. He wanted to buy our ranch and offered a fair price. My father was present, and he told them bluntly that his ranch was not for sale, and it never would be. Ty butted in and said to my father in very disrespectful words that he should give serious thought to selling or our ranch may go bankrupt."

"That's a threat, and he could be arrested for that statement," Dallas said.

"Did Bill Denton say anything to his son?"

"Yes, he told Ty that he had said enough and his father pulled him back away from us. Ty glared at us, and I saw the hate in his eyes. As they left, the man from Texas and Bill Denton did tell us thanks for our time and to reconsider their offer."

Dallas rubbed his hand over his chin. "Ty is the problem as I see it. The father is a businessman who is not doing anything that is against the law. We may not like him for being rich, but he has the right to ask. Of course, you and your father are justified by not permitting them on your property. Maybe you and your father should get with Romon and the other neighbouring ranchers and share the problems with them that Bill Denton is stirring up."

"That is what my father told me. Yes, that is a good idea about getting the small Mexican ranchers together. He and my mother are in town grocery shopping and buying supplies. He told me that if you visited us, he welcomes you to come here and visit us anytime."

"I like your father. He is a real cowboy and a gentleman. I better get to going and finish my business. Rest assured, the sheriff and I have our eyes on Ty Denton. Thanks for the coffee and delicious cookies, Victoria."

Near the turnoff to Diablo Ridge, Dallas saw a pickup truck parked alongside the road with both the drivers and passenger doors open. *That's Pablo Morales' truck.* He swung the Jeep over and stopped in front of the truck, jumped out and hurried to the passenger side where he saw Pablo leaning over his wife. They both had blood on their faces and their clothing.

"Here, let me help you," Dallas said, as he placed his hand on Pablo's shoulder. Pablo's wife was conscious and had deep cuts to her face. Dallas pulled out a clean handkerchief from his Jean pocket and began blotting the wounds on her face. He turned to Pablo, who also had cuts and bruises on his face.

Dallas removed the cell phone from his jacket pocket. Pablo put his hand on the phone. "No, please do not call 911."

"Why not, you both need medical assistance."

"The men told me if I contacted the sheriff, they would come after my family and us. Can you please help us get to back to our ranch?"

"Who did this to you?" Dallas asked.

"I don't know. They wore those funny masks with holes for their eyes and mouth. I could not recognise them."

"How many men were there?"

"Two, two men, one large man and a slender man who appeared to be much younger than the other one."

"Can you drive?" Dallas asked Pablo.

"Yes, I can drive okay."

"Drive back to your ranch. I will follow you." Dallas helped Pablo into the driver's seat and made his wife as comfortable as possible in the passenger seat.

Antonio went into a rage when he and Dallas helped his parents into the house. Victoria tended to their wounds and gave them water to drink.

"Why would anyone want to hurt my mother and father? They have never hurt anyone in their lives. I want to find them and pay them back for what they did."

"We have no clue as to who did this," Dallas said, trying to calm Antonio down. "My guess is that it has something to do with wanting to buy your ranch, and that would be with the Dentons."

"I'm going to the Denton ranch and beat the holy crap out of Ty Denton," Antonio blurted out.

Dallas replied, "If I knew it was him that did this, I would go with you. If you touched the son, his dad would have you locked up. Let me do more investigating into who assaulted your parents. I am getting closer to finding out who hired a hitman to kill Carlos. It seems to me like wanting to buy out you ranchers, and the people like yourself and the Garcias are the primary targets."

Antonio agreed, but he was still angry about his parents being assaulted. "Thanks for helping my mother and father. You are a good man, Mr McCall."

Dallas suppressed a grin.

Dallas drove away from the Morales ranch for the second time today, both times the subject revolved around the Dentons.

Damn, that pisses me off that those two nice people got assaulted. I think it might have been Badger and Weasel who beat them up. Now, to find out if they were the ones. My guess is that Ty Denton had something to do with the assault.

Dallas drove to the Garcia ranch to inform them about what happened to their neighbours and to warn them against Bill Denton and representatives from a Texas investment company.

"My parents are in town," Carla said when Dallas climbed out of the Jeep. "Come inside, and we can talk."

In the Garcia ranch kitchen, Carla agreed with Dallas about getting all of the Mexican ranchers together for a meeting and to share information about the attempts to buy their properties.

"I will get with my father and arrange a meeting. I will let you know when a meeting is arranged."

Carla walked with Dallas to his Jeep. "I've missed you," she said. "Are you still seeing Lori?"

He smiled hardily at her. "Yes, I am." Dallas watched her eyes become moist. "You are still my favorite cowgirl."

She raised her head quickly, the moisture in her eyes turned to fire. "Damn, you, McCall... Damn you for not giving me a chance to show you how much I love and respect you."

Dallas pulled her to him holding her while she burst into broken sobs. She whispered, her breath warm in his ear, her body pushing firmly against his, "I want you."

Dallas raised her tear filled face up and kissed her firmly on the lips. "I can't resist you any longer. Take me to your bedroom."

Their lovemaking was wild and hot. Carla moaned and cried out, "You are my first, oh, I love it, and I love you."

They laid exhausted in each other's arms. Carla whispered, "You make me feel incredible. Where did you learn all these things?"

Dallas laughed softly and kissed her. "I went to sex school."

"You did not." She bit him gently on his ear.

"We better get our clothes on and get out of here before your parents come home," Dallas said.

She moved her body on top of him. "They will not be home for a couple of more hours."

On the drive back to town, Dallas felt ashamed that he had given in to Carla's beauty, and he had betrayed, Lori. *Well, Lori and I are not really a couple. We're not engaged or going steady so to speak. I'm just a two-timing cowboy who happens to like two women at the same time.*

Chapter 22

It was ten minutes to six that late afternoon when Lori met Dallas at the front door of her house. "Come in, cowboy. You must be hungry after being out on the range all day."

"I'm always hungry, you know that. Herding chickens is hard work," he grinned. *Yeah, McCall, you've been making love with Carla, now you are face to face with Lori, who I think loves me. I made a mistake, sorry Lori. It will never happen again.*

She kissed him. "I love your sense of humor. You make me laugh."

"I make myself laugh sometimes."

Lori took hold of Dallas' hand and led him into the dining room.

The grandparents made Dallas feel welcome, and with their wit and personalities, they reminded him of his grandparents back in Texas.

Grandpa Porter eyed Dallas with steel gray eyes, a stern look on his aged face. "Son, Lori tells me you are in search of whoever killed your friend. This is the first time a person has been murdered around her in decades. The last time was when a rancher and his son were killed during a dispute over water rights. Not getting into your business, but most of the fights have been and still are over land and water rights. That's more than I've said in ten years." A grin crossed his wrinkled face.

Dallas smiled, "Thank you, sir, for your wisdom and advice. I have come to find out that what you said is the absolute truth. I may be in over my head being an outsider, but when my friend was murdered by cowards, I could not stand by and wait for the law to bring the responsible people to justice. I must have the old Texas wild west take charge in my blood."

Grandpa Porter chuckled and held up his wine glass. "Here's to the way it used to be and should be today. Good luck to you, Dallas McCall."

The toast brought moisture to Dallas' eyes.

Lori came to Dallas' rescue. "Is anyone ready for dessert and coffee?"

Dallas and Grandmother Porter said, "Yes, please," at the same time. That brought laughter to all four of them.

"Thanks for the wonderful evening and delicious meal," Dallas said, as he stood by Lori at the front door.

Grandma, sitting in her wheelchair in the family room near the door, smiled. "When you come back again, and I hope it will be soon...I will fry up a couple of chickens and bake an apple pie. How does that sound?"

"Um, I love fried chicken and apple pie. Thank you, ma'am," Dallas replied, with a big grin on his face.

Lori walked with Dallas to the Jeep. She put her arms around his neck. "I want you to please be careful when you're out on the prairie and mountain roads. I worry about you all of the time."

"I'm always careful. Don't worry your pretty self about me. I am getting close to finding out the truth and who is responsible for Carlos' death. I really do like and care for you. I hope you know that."

"Like me, you just like me is that all?" she said, her voice trailing off.

Dallas kissed her. "I like you, and I also like you more."

She hit him in the stomach. "I guess that will do. I'll get you loosened up one of these days. Now get some rest and stop by and see me tomorrow. Remember, I love you – Got it?"

"Yes, I hear you. I will never forget that, ever."

They kissed again, and Dallas gently broke away, climbed in the Jeep and drove away waving a hand over his head. *Damn, I'm happy being with Lori and I feel so lousy cheating on her by having an affair with Carla. I'm not good enough for her. I need to break off my relationship with both, Lori and Carla; that will solve my problem.*

Back in his room, Dallas removed his boots and laid down on the bed, his arms behind his head. He thought about how hard the early days must have been for the Mexican ranchers fighting for their right to live on the land that their ancestors ranched for years before them. I understand how it would be in Texas where my parent's ranch is located if they were being strong-armed to sell the land that has been in our family for generations. The Mexican ranchers can't just sell and walk away from their homes; it's their livelihood, and it's what they want to pass down to their children.

I hope Romon organises a meeting with his neighbours soon. The longer they wait, the more difficult it will be for them.

Chapter 23

A knock on the front door awakened Carla Garcia at the break of dawn. She struggled out of bed, through on her housecoat and walked to the door rubbing the sleep from her eyes. *Whoever that is must know us. Maybe it is Dallas stopping by for an early morning breakfast.*

As she neared the door, she saw the shadowy figure of a large man blocking the light coming from the porch peeking into the window next to the door. She unlocked the bolt and opened the door to find two men wearing ski masks standing there.

"What do you want?" she yelled out.

The larger man said in a deeply disguised voice, "This is a warning; you Mexicans are not wanted in this valley. Sell your property and get out or you will pay the consequences." They both turned and hurried off into the early morning darkness.

Carla stepped out on the porched and yelled. "I know it is you John Badger, you're too stupid to try and cover up your ugly face. Dallas McCall will be making another visit to you. You had better get your ass out of town before he comes for you." She couldn't help but laugh out loud.

It was seven-thirty when Dallas received the call from Carla telling him about what happened.

"I'll be out to see you after I eat breakfast. Are you okay?"

"Yes, I am doing all right. I told my dad that it was a lost traveller asking for directions at our door earlier this morning. I don't want him to have more worries than what he already has."

"See you shortly." Dallas disconnected the call. *Damn, I hate what is going on with all of the hate going on toward the Mexican people.*

Romon, Carla, Rosa and Christian sat at the kitchen table eating breakfast when Dallas arrived.

Carla poured Dallas a cup of coffee and sat a breakfast taco in front of him. He smiled, "Thanks, I like a second breakfast."

"What brings you out this way on such an early morning?" Romon asked.

Dallas glanced at Carla and saw her raise her eyebrows. "I was going to the Morales Ranch and speak with Antonio. Since you were so near and I knew Rosa would have a pot of coffee on and possibly tacos for breakfast. I took you up on your offer to stop by anytime." He winked at Christian and smiled.

There was laughter around the table.

Carla said, "We are always happy to see you."

"Me too," Christian said in between bites of his taco, his eyes on Dallas.

"I better get moving and let you cattle ranchers get on with your business. Thanks for breakfast, Rosa," Dallas said, as he stood up from his chair. He shook Romon's hand and winked at Christian.

"I'll walk you to your Jeep," Carla said.

She told Dallas about the early morning visitors and how easy it was to recognise John Badger and probably his friend, Weasel.

Dallas smiled, "They had to be paid to be so dumb thinking you would not know who they were. My guess is Bill Denton is trying the strong-arm tactics and trying to scare your dad to sell the ranch. This time, I will run them out of town. I am near finding enough evidence on Denton to turn over to the sheriff."

"Thanks, for looking out for us. You are such a good friend. We all love you; I love you more. I loved being with you and us making love together."

"Carlos would appreciate our friendship and respect your love for me. You need to forget about our time together; I'm not the man for you. I got to run. Let me know if you have any more trouble."

"Yes, you are the man for me and the man I want. Come and see me," Carla said, her smile was bright and shinning.

"I will. Let me know if you need an extra cowpuncher. I know that this time of the year a cattle ranch is mighty busy."

"I could use the help, but I know how occupied you are."

"I will always make time for you."

"Dad and I are riding to the western sector early tomorrow morning and drive the cattle we have there back to the grassland behind the pond." Her smile was radiant and innocent.

"Oh," Romon said, "I have a meeting arranged with all of the Mexican ranchers Saturday at one o'clock. Carla told me you stopped by and told her about your idea. Thanks for thinking about us."

"Great," Dallas replied, "I'll see you bright and early tomorrow morning ready to cowboy."

"Thank you, cowboy. Adios," Carla said.

By eleven o'clock that morning, Dallas located Badger and Weasel at the M&J Café drinking beer and filling their mouths with Nachos. When Dallas stormed through the door, not a person in the dining room stirred, there was dead silence.

Without saying a word, Dallas walked to Badger and with a powerful right-hand punch, he struck him in the face so hard that he tumbled over backward and lay unconscious on the hard floor. Weasel raised up from his chair to run, and Dallas caught him by his shirt collar and slammed him to the floor following up with a swift kick to the side of his face. Badger was making gurgling noises in his throat as he attempted to get up from the floor. Dallas moved swiftly to the fallen Badger and slammed his boot down on his chest.

Dallas's voice was loud and firm when he said, "Badger, you and your little Weasel buddy have two hours to collect your personal belongings and get your asses out of town. If I find you have not left town, I will come for you and assist you both with your new relocation. You will not be happy with where I take you. Now, get the hell out of here. Do not go near the Garcia ranch. I promise you if you do, Romon Garcia will shoot you on site."

Dallas followed the two out of the restaurant and watched them climb into Badgers Ford Bronco and drive away toward the west.

"That should be the last I see of those two cowards," Dallas said out loud.

The next morning, Carla, Romon and Dallas were in the saddle by the time the sun rose. Dallas could not help but notice that Romon was a real Mexican rancher. His jeans were torn at the knees, his work boots were broken-down and he had cuts and scratches on his hands. His face was weary after long days in the saddle. *I respect that man so much. Carlos was proud of his dad, and Romon was proud of his son.*

It was four-thirty that afternoon when the five-hundred head of prime beef was grazing in the pasture. Dallas felt great getting back to the cowboy life he loved so much.

Dallas joined the family for happy hour and dinner. Romon and Carla remarked on what a good cowboy Dallas was and how thankful they were for him volunteering to help them.

Romon said, "Carlos wrote in one of his letters to us that he had the feeling that you would eventually go back to Texas and then return to cattle ranching."

After dinner, the family walked with Dallas to his Jeep.

"We will see you Saturday at one o'clock for the meeting," Romon said, before Dallas walked out to where his Jeep was parked.

"I'll be there. See you then. Thanks again for dinner, Rosa and Carla."

It was seven o'clock, and he was on his way back to his room entirely exhausted from a day's work as a cowboy. *I'm beat all to hell, but I loved getting back in the saddle. I haven't had time to think much of my home and family in Texas. I'm going back when I finish what I set out to do. I think Carlos would approve of me joining my family.*

"We will see you Saturday at one o'clock for the meeting," Romon said, before Dallas walked out to his Jeep.

"I'll be there. See you then."

The room was dark and quiet, as Dallas's mind drifted back to the night mission raids he went on in Afghanistan, and the ghosts that haunted him and the terrifying things happened during his combat tours. *I plan to remain secretive about my role in the war, and not burden my family with the horrors of war. Carlos told me about a mission that I sent his platoon on seeing strange, ghostly figures in the desert. He told me about claiming that his unit was plagued by a mysterious phantom that would appear around the outskirts of their positions and vanish in the blink of an eye. I remember him saying to me that he felt the phantom was out to kill him. He was really freaked out. I wonder if there is any truth to a mysterious force that killed Carlos?*

Dallas placed his hands on the sides of his head and cried out, "Go away, leave me alone and let me live in peace."

Chapter 24

On Saturday, the Garcia ranch parking area was filling up with pickup trucks and SUVs as the neighboring Mexican ranchers gathered to discuss the situation they encountered with Bill Denton and outside investment companies wanting to buy their ranches.

Carla opened the meeting for her father. "Thank you, friends and neighbours for coming today and sharing our viewpoints on the recent push by the Denton Ranch and investment companies from Texas. They are in competition to buy our land to be used for recreational ranches, such as dude ranches and hunting clubs. We all have been contacted by one or more of the companies along with Bill Denton. Their offers are much lower than what our ranches are worth. Our families have been landowners in this county since the 1800 hundreds, and we have no intentions of selling our homestead."

Antonio Morales agreed, "My father and I will never sell our ranch at any price. My parents were assaulted by local employees of Bill Denton. Our good friend, Dallas McCall, took the law in his own hands and tracked down and dealt harshly with the men who hurt my family. We will fight if necessary to keep our land as cattle ranches and not dude ranches."

Miguel Mendoza spoke next, "I totally agree with Antonio and his father and the Garcia family. I am fortunate to have one of the largest ranches, and I will not sell one single acre to anyone for any reason. I stand firm with the rest of you."

Dallas spoke with the ranch owners and assured them that the County Sheriff was fully aware of the situation and he supported their rights not to be forced to sell their land.

Every head in the room turned to the front door as Bill Denton, and his son, Ty, entered. They both removed their hats, and Bill spoke, "I know that we are not welcome here, but we wanted to address all of you about a proposal. If I may, Mr Garcia?"

Romon glanced around the room at the facial expressions of his neighboring ranchers. There were puzzled looks on their faces.

"Let's hear what you have to say, Mr Denton," Romon said in an angry voice.

Bill managed a slight smile. "Thank you. It has come to our attention that my son, Ty and I have been unfair to many of you here. We wanted to buy land along with investors to build hunting resorts located in the valley. Our goal was to bring added income to our ranches; and yes, to the Denton ranch. After Ty and I saw what the Texas stranger, Mr Dallas McCall is trying to accomplish by finding out who murdered his friend and the son of Mr and Mrs Garcia, and why he was killed, we took another look at our mistakes, and the methods we used in an attempt to buy up your land…"

"Hold on, Mr Denton," Antonio Morales yelled. "Is what I hear you say is that you want us to go along with selling our ranch land to you."

Bill replied, "No, not exactly. If you permit me to finish, I will provide you with more information."

Romon took another look around the room and saw the ranchers whispering to each other and nodding their heads in agreement.

"Please, Mr Denton. Proceed," Romon said.

"Thank you," Bill said. "We propose that we all, each of us ranch owners pool portions of our land and legally form an association that will bring stability and lifetime income for our families and our future generations. I have spoken with my attorney, and we can establish an association where we all will be equal partners. Ty came up with a suggested name for our venture. *Little Creek Ranchers Association.* I cannot blame any of you for not trusting us for the way my family has been acting toward you for the past years. We want to be your friends and live in peace with our families and friends."

The room was utterly silent as the attendees exchanged glances and whispered between each other. Then there was a clapping of hands coming from Miguel Mendoza.

Miguel said, "I believe Mr Denton has a valid proposal and we should take a long hard look at what our future will be. We will share 50,000 acres of our prime land to the association if it is approved."

One by one, the ranchers agreed to meet again, along with attorneys and to officially form the association.

Romon spoke with Carla and Dallas, "What do you two think about what Bill proposed?"

"It's not my business," Dallas said. "I do think you need to think about his idea in a positive way. He sounds sincere to me."

"Yes, I agree with Dallas," Carla said softly.

Romon addressed the attendees, "We have a good feeling about your proposal, Mr Denton. I go along with the suggestion that we all meet again with attorneys present and vote on the issue."

"We agree with you," Antonio replied.

The vote was unanimous.

Bill and Ty Denton remained for a short time, speaking with the ranchers and shaking hands.

The meeting was adjourned, and Dallas stayed and visited with the Garcias. After not much pressure, he accepted the invitation to stay and have dinner with them.

"I think that the meeting went well," Dallas said during dinner.

"Yes, I do too," Romon replied. "By us all grouping together, we make a strong force that will protect us from the outsiders wanting our ranches. I am so pleased to see the old Bill Denton that I saw years ago. His son, Ty, appears different. I think he may have finally grown up."

The golden sunset lingered over the distant mountains as Dallas drove back to Little Creek. Dallas felt a loneliness fall over him as he thought about Carlos and what he must have gone through during the last minutes of his life. He could not resist the hatred he had for whoever killed Carlos. It would not go away.

Chapter 25

It was another glorious New Mexico chilly autumn morning when Dallas started the Jeep and checked the gas gauge. *Three-quarters of a tank should do me today as I'm not sure where or what I am going to do. I haven't heard from Ivanna in quite a while. I should call her, but her husband may be near her phone and think we are having an affair. I don't understand why she is secretive about what her son told her about Ty Denton hiring someone to kill Carlos. She is aggressive about me helping her with her husband's view on selling to outsiders wanting to buy out local Mexican ranchers. Now I don't know about her or trust her as I have been since our first meeting!*

Talk about ESP. Dallas's cell phone buzzed. It was Ivanna.

"This is McCall, hello, Ivanna."

"Hello, Dallas. We need to talk."

"Sure, where at and when?"

"The best location for me is where we have been meeting at Diablo Ridge. I do my morning ride on my ATV, and no one ever suspects that I am meeting you."

"Okay, I can be there in thirty minutes. How will that work for you?"

"Yes, that is perfect. See you soon." She disconnected the call.

I wonder what the hell she is up to. Guess I'll find out soon.

Dallas drove over the familiar road that he had travelled so many times to Diablo Ridge faster than usual wanting to meet Ivanna and find out what was so important. She was waiting for him when he stopped the Jeep near where she sat on her ATV.

When Ivanna climbed off of the ATV and removed her helmet, she was in tears.

Dallas moved to her and waited for her to talk. "It's Deigo. He and his father got into a heated argument early this morning, and Deigo drove away in his pickup with a suitcase and his hunting rifle." The tears rolled down her cheeks.

Wanting to pull her to him and console her, but he decided not to. "I don't want to get wrapped up in your family problems. What do you think I could do to help the situation?"

She looked at him with a confused look on her face. "Well, I was hoping you would find him before he does something stupid."

"Stupid; what do you mean by doing something stupid?"

Tears continued flowing down her cheeks. She wiped the tears away with the back of her hand. Her mouth quivered as she tried to speak. "He…he told his father that he was going to meet Ty Denton, and they were going to Mexico and never coming back. Miguel is heartbroken and too stubborn to go after Diego. Ty is no good and a troublemaker. Can't you please help me?"

"Maybe. Under one condition. I get your husband's approval to go after your son."

"I'm afraid he will not approve of you going after our son. He knows that it is his job to go after Diego."

"Then I don't go. You should go back to your ranch, and hopefully; your son will think things over and return. I have no reason to go looking for Diego, Ty, yes; because I don't think Diego had anything to do with Carlos's murder."

Ivanna looked at Dallas, her eyes filling with more tears. "I believe Ty killed Carlos and I don't think Diego knows that. My…son is in danger. Please, Dallas, help me, I beg you."

Dallas gave her a sharp look. "Lady, if you are making up a story just so I will pursue your runaway son then you got me all wrong. You and your husband have a problem son, and you need to deal with it, and do not involve me in your family quarrels."

"I'm telling you the truth. A long-time ranch hand told me that Ty bragged about shooting Carlos and getting rid of the one person keeping him from being a millionaire."

"Okay, I'm not convinced, but I'll think about it. What kind and what color of a truck is Diego driving?"

"A silver 2017 Dodge Ram, four-door crew cab."

"I will call you if I find out where he is. I may not confront him if I find him. I will let you know where he is, and you and your husband can do the rest. Do you understand my conditions?"

"Yes, thank you." She stepped up to Dallas and kissed him, turned and climbed aboard her ATV, put on her helmet and sped away.

What in the hell have I got myself into this time? It may work out on my side if I catch up with Ty Denton and find out more about what is going on between him and Diego. The Diego kid, I don't know about him; he's weird. I do know that whoever killed Carlos was staring him in the eyes. It is possible one of these two could have killed Carlos. Why? That's why I have to find out who it was. I may be on the right track by finding these two so-called friends and what they are up doing. Since the rancher's meeting at the Garcia ranch with Bill and Ty Denton present, I got the feeling that Ty may not be involved with Carlos' death. He may be doing a great acting job!

Dallas took off driving down from the ridge and headed west, taking a chance that he may find Diego still at the Denton ranch looking for Ty and he has not taken off towards Mexico.

Twenty-five minutes later, Dallas's decision to go to the Denton ranch was correct. Outside the gate leading to the ranch house, he saw Diego's pickup parked next to Ty's truck. As he neared them, he saw Diego knock Ty to the ground holding a rifle to Ty's chest. *Damn, what in the hell is going on with those two?*

Diego turned his head toward the speeding oncoming Jeep and ran to his truck and sped away in the opposite direction away from Dallas, his truck kicking up rocks and dirt as he gained speed and disappeared over the hills.

As Dallas stopped the Jeep, Ty raised up from the gravel and stood looking toward where the fleeing pickup truck disappeared. "Goddam crazy bastard threatened to kill me," Ty screamed.

Dallas was by his side and asked him if he was hurt.

"No, only my pride. I let him get the drop on me, and he sucker punched me."

"What did he hit you for? You said he threatened to kill you?"

"Yeah, he did. We got into an argument about him wanting me to go with him to Mexico. I told him that I had no reason to go with him. He went off on a rave about why I wasn't his friend, and I was backing out on going into an agreement with him to buy the Garcia ranch, and siding with my father and Mexican ranchers to form the association that would save our land. He's frigging nuts. What are you doing here?"

Dallas said, "His mother wants me to bring him back to their ranch. I'm going after him. Do you want to go with me?"

"Yeah, I want to kick his ass. I'll go with you."

"Climb your ass in the Jeep," Dallas said. "Any idea where he may be headed?"

"My guess is Diablo Ridge. He always goes there when he is pouting or depressed."

The Jeep bucked and swerved as Dallas cut around the main road and took a shortcut around the rocky ridges, hoping to get to Diablo Ridge before Diego if that was where he was headed.

Dallas yelled over the noise of the Jeep. "I am going to ask you straight up. Did you kill Carlos?"

Ty turned his head sharply to face Dallas. "No, hell no. I had nothing to do with his death. We had our differences, but we were friends until Diego got between us with wanting to buy the Garcia family ranch."

"I now think Diego killed Carlos. Do you know if he did?"

"I'm not sure, but he bragged about getting Carlos out of the way. He was jealous of Carlos, and his friendship with him turned to hate after Carlos returned home after his discharge from the Marines."

"There is his truck parked at the bottom of the ridge. He beat us here and is at his favourite spot at the peak of the ridge," Ty yelled.

Suddenly, the sound of a gun cracked, and a bullet hummed close to Dallas's head, then two more shots rang out, and the bullets hit the back of the Jeep. Dallas turned sharply and pulled to a stop near a cluster of rocks. Rapid shots began hitting around them, hitting the Jeep windshield sending glass flying over Dallas and Ty.

Dallas pulled his pistol from his waistband. Out of the corner of his eye, he was aware of movement along the ridge above them. "This 9mm is not much of a match for whatever Diego is shooting at us with. He is using a semiautomatic rifle, or there are two shooters. "

"He is using his Winchester .308 hunting rifle with a scope which is not semiautomatic. Be aware, he is a deadly shot." Ty kneeled lower to the ground as two more rounds hit the rocks next to him. "He's targeting me," Ty screamed.

"Yeah, I've got to get behind whoever is up there, or they will kill us both. More bullets were coming from another rifle beside Diego's Winchester. Sounds to me like someone is shooting an AR-15. I know this area pretty damn good by now. You stay hidden where you are, and I will move around behind us and make my way up on the ridge behind them."

Dallas heard more gunfire, and another round of bullets that hit close to his ear, and as they struck the rocks, it made a singing sound. "Damn, that boy and whoever is with him is damn sure trying to kill us."

Then another shot rang out, and Ty screamed and rolled backward. "I'm hit, oh lord, my arm." He grabbed hold of Dallas's coat sleeve and cried, "Am I going to die?"

Blood spilled out from Ty's jacket covering the rocks beneath where he laid screaming, "My arm, I'm going to die, help me."

"Be calm, you are not going to die," Dallas told him. Dallas quickly jumped into action as he had done while in battle with the Marines. He removed Ty's belt from his jeans, removed his blood-soaked jacket and applied a tourniquet to stop the bleeding. Dallas moved him underneath the Jeep to keep him out of the line of fire coming from the deadly fire on the ridge.

"Stay put and don't move," Dallas ordered. He gave the injured, frightened young cowboy a slight smile and then he crept behind the Jeep and was soon out of sight.

Shots continued to ring out around the Jeep as Dallas moved quickly, quietly and undetected around the ridge toward the shooter's position similar to what he did as a Marine Recon Scout in Afghanistan with his raider team.

As he crept over the top of the ridge, he spotted Diego lying prone on his stomach, his rifle resting on a flat rock, the barrel aimed down towards the Jeep. Next to him, kneeling and shooting at the Jeep where Ty laid wounded was the hulking figure of John Badger.

"Goddamn you, John Badger," Dallas muttered under his breath. He took a defensive stance facing the shooters. He yelled out over the booming sounds of the rifles. "Drop your weapons and put your hands in the air."

Badger quickly turned and pointed his AR-15 at Dallas. He yelled out in his loud raspy voice, "Goodbye, stranger."

The anger built up in Dallas for his dislike of John Badger. Badger no sooner got the words out of his mouth when Dallas, his piercing blue eyes filled with hate put two bullets from his 9mm pistol into the chest of John Badger. The force of the bullets knocked him backward, landing on the hard rocks on Diablo Ridge.

Diego jumped up to his feet and pointed his rifle at Dallas.

"Make a move, and I will be more than happy to blow your head off." Dallas quickly walked up to him and grabbed the rifle and sat in down behind him. He grabbed Diego by the collar of his jacket and threw him against the rocky wall.

Diego began to whimper and cry, "Please don't kill me, I am begging you, please don't kill me."

"Shut up that damn crying. I should fill you full of holes and throw your sorry ass off of this ridge. You and now that dead, sorry son of a bitch, John Badger killed my friend," Dallas's voice filled the mountain air with his cry of anger.

Diego stopped crying, and a changed expression came over his face. "I hope Denton is dead. I want him dead, just as I wanted Garcia to die. They both looked down their noses at me and made fun of me because I am gay. I wanted to join the Marines, but Carlos told me they would not let gays enlist. I hated him for that. He had all the friends hanging around him all the time. My friend, John Badger and I, followed him to Diablo Ridge in broad daylight that day in August, and we shot him with my deer rifle and Badger's AR-15 from the ridge. Then we walked down to where he laid bleeding from the wounds we put in his body. As Carlos lay bleeding, he threatened to kick my ass. I then laughed at him and put a bullet in his head. Ty Denton betrayed me and told my mother that I was gay, and then she told my father. They all hate me – everyone hates me except John Badger. I wanted them all dead." He then switched back to his crying personality.

The boy is crazy, but he still is a killer. I hope he makes the same confession to the sheriff.

Dallas used Diego's belt from his jeans to bind his hands behind his back.

Dallas called Sheriff Dan Baker on his cell phone and told him what happened, and that John Badger was dead. He rushed

Ty to the doctor in Little Creek and turned Diego over to Sheriff Dan Baker. Diego repeated the story to Dan about how and why he, along with John Badger, ambushed and murdered Carlos.

Diego screamed and cried from his cell. Dan recorded his vocal rampage telling how he and John Badger murdered Carlos repeatedly. He made the same statement when the county prosecutor arrived and continued yelling and screaming how he murdered Carlos with his attorney and parents present.

Dan said, "Well, Dallas McCall. You are a born detective. You worked on the Carlos Garcia case like a professional. I can get you appointed to a deputy sheriff job if you like."

Dallas grinned. "Thanks, Dan. I'm not so sure that I can follow the rules of the law if I was your deputy. Besides, I did not know John Badger and Diego were friends, and together they cowardly murdered Carlos in cold blood."

"I hope you have good insurance," Dallas said to Lori as he drove the Jeep with a shattered windshield and bullet holes in the body into her open garage stall.

"My Lord, what happened to you?" she said with panic in her voice.

"It's a long story. I'll tell you later over dinner. Dan Baker and his wife have invited us to have dinner with them. I'll keep the location a surprise."

Lori giggled. "Don't tell me you two are going to cook?"

"Cook. I have you know that I am a good cook. No, I'm not going to cook dinner, we are dining out." A warm smile lit up his eyes.

Lori looked at Dallas and smiled. "You're a silly man, you make me laugh. Being with you, talking with you and laughing with you, that's what I adore most about you."

"Thanks. You made the right choice of permitting me to love you."

Lori came to him, placed her arms around his neck and kissed him passionately. "I love you, cowboy."

Chapter 26

That evening was all you can eat taco night at the M&J café. Dallas and Lori, along with Sheriff Dan Baker and his wife, Sally, sat at a large table in the corner of the dining room eating beef tacos, drinking beer and carrying on a conversation about how their town had changed since Dallas arrived in September.

"Maybe I'll stick around and run for mayor," Dallas said laughing.

Dan said, "You would make a good one, but a better deputy sheriff."

"No, not me. I'm just a cowboy at heart, and that will probably be my calling in life."

Lori chimed in, "You're a good man, Dallas McCall, whatever you decide to do with your life. I only hope I am included!"

Dallas gave her a strange, admiring glance then smiled at her. "You will."

Sally said in a friendly tone of voice, "I am so happy to finally meet you, Dallas. Dan has spoken highly of you, which is not is a normal trait. It must be that you two are former Marines."

"You're ruining my tough sheriff image. McCall may think that I like him." Dan gave Dallas a glance and winked at him. He smiled at his wife and Lori.

"The feeling is mutual," Dallas said. "We both have tough guy images, but our respect for our country, families, and friends have a weak spot in our hearts."

"Amen," Dan said softly. "I hate to break this up, but I have a night patrol to make sure all the bad guys are asleep and not out causing trouble."

The two couples bid good night to each other and went their separate ways. Lori convinced Dallas to spend the night with her. It didn't take much convincing on his part.

Dallas fell against the dresser, attempting to pull his boots off while Lori was tugging at his jeans. He laughed, "Grandpa will be up here with a shotgun if he hears all of the noise we're making trying to get our clothes off."

Lori giggled. "Not to worry. I told him and Grandma that I might have you sleepover since I was no longer a teenager and this was my house."

"Great, now help me with these boots so I can get you in bed."

The next morning, Dallas sat smiling on a kitchen stool, drinking coffee and watching Lori standing at the stove frying eggs wearing a short housecoat.

She turned her head and smiled. "What are you thinking about, cowboy?"

"You, I'm thinking about how happy you make me feel. I would like a night like we had to last forever. Oh, what is under your housecoat?"

She smiled. "Nothing. Are you proposing to me?"

"Oh, I don't know. Maybe, oh, hell. I'm thinking about it. You're naked?"

Lori laughed. "Yes, I am naked. When you decide if you want me to marry you, I would appreciate it if you let me know."

Dallas had a sheepish look on his face. "Are those eggs about ready?"

She shrugged her shoulders, "Maybe." Then she turned and placed a plate filled with eggs, bacon, hash browns and toast in front of Dallas. She kissed him, smiled and returned to the stove.

"Thank you, sweetheart."

"You're welcome, sweetheart. After you get your stomach full, I will show you what is underneath my housecoat that you are so interested in." Her face was filled with joy and love. She gave him a mischievous smile and raised her eyebrows.

Dallas laid his silverware on the plate and moved swiftly and picked Lori up in his arms and carried her to the bedroom.

Thanksgiving Day
November 22, 2018

Grandma Porter hummed a tune as she helped Lori prepare the Thanksgiving dinner while sitting in her wheelchair at the kitchen table. Grandpa and Dallas sat in the family room watching football. The Chicago Bears played the Detroit Lions in the first game, and Dallas was waiting for his namesake team, the Dallas Cowboys to play against the Washington Redskins.

Lori pushed her grandmother into the family room and stopped her wheelchair next to her husband. Lori sat down next to Dallas on the couch. "Another thirty-minutes and dinner will be ready," Lori said.

"Good, I'm starved," Grandpa Porter said. "Thanksgiving is a family tradition. It should include things you eat and enjoy the rest of the year as well, not just the one day."

"Amen to that, sir," Dallas replied. "I am honoured you asked me to share this special day with you. It is a time to be with family. I missed quite a few holidays with family when I was in the Marines."

"We are happy to have you with us," Grandma Porter said.

"I second that," Lori said, smiling and placing her hand on Dallas's hand.

"Is that the timer I heard ringing?" Grandpa Porter said.

During dinner, Lori's grandparents talked with her about them moving to an assisted living facility in Santa Fe. Grandpa said, "We are aging very fast, and our medical conditions are not improving as you can tell, Lori. With only one doctor in town and the nearest hospital is over thirty miles away, we need to get serious and make our move."

"Oh, I agree with you," Lori replied. "You are not a burden to me, and I think you both know that."

Grandpa said, "We do, and we love you, and we want you to have a life besides taking care of us in this little out of the way town. You should give thought to selling out the garage and this house and move to Santa Fe with us. You have the education and the youth to make a good life for yourself."

Lori with a smile across her face raised her wine glass. "To our future and good health. God bless you, Grandma and Grandpa."

Dallas joined in the salute, "My respect and well wishes to each of you."

"And to you, Dallas McCall," Lori said cheerfully.

On Monday morning, Lori contacted a realtor from Santa Fe and placed her business and house up for sale. She also made arrangements to have her grandparents moved to Santa Fe.

Dallas assisted Lori with her projects, and the two spent every day and night together. "I smell love in the air," Lori said to Dallas.

He smiled and took her hands in his. "Oh, do you?"

Lori playfully slapped his hands and tilted her head slightly to the side. "Yes, I do."

Chapter 27

December 2018

The trial for Diego Mendoza lasted for two weeks. After a hard fight by the Mendoza family's lawyer attempts to prove Diego was innocent due to mental illness, the prosecutor's case was strong, and the jury found Diego an accomplish with John Badger, guilty of the murder of Carlos Garcia. He was sentenced to fifty years to life in the state prison at Santa Fe.

Miguel and Ivanna met with long-time friends, the Garcia family for lunch after the trial. Miguel said in a near whisper, "We feel horrible about Diego murdering Carlos, and we are so ashamed. We can never repay you for your loss. The secret friendship between Diego and John Badger went undetected, and we are sorry we never found out about the influence John Badger was putting on our son."

Romon replied, "You are our friends, and it was not your fault what Diego did. Our hearts go out to you both as you deal with your sorrow and move on with your lives."

Dallas declined the 10,000 dollar award put up by Miguel Mendoza for the arrest and conviction of Carlos' killer, their son, Diego. Dallas requested the money be donated to the city of Little Creek to help bring the historical town back to the life it once had.

Bill Denton and his son, Ty, matched the 10,000-dollar reward that Miguel Mendoza offered and opened a bank account in the name of Carlos Garcia for 20,000 dollars to be used for school supplies in the Little Creek elementary and high school.

Saturday, December 15
The Garcia Ranch

Carla invited Dallas and Lori to have dinner with the Garcia family and to give thanks to Dallas for finding and capturing the person who killed Carlos.

During the drive to the ranch, Lori said, "I am surprised that Carla invited me to come with you to her house. I know she has the hots for you."

Dallas smiled at Lori. "She knows that you and I are together. You two were friends before I came along and I hope that you both remain friends."

"We will as far as I am concerned. I have always liked and respected Carla."

Dallas kept thinking of what he would say to the family now that his mission to Little Creek was finished. *I will just go on being myself and try to move on with my life along with continuing friendship with the Garcia family and my relationship with Lori. It does make me sad to leave Carla. I do like her, and if it was not for my love for Lori, we could probably have a long-time relationship. Another life, McCall. You made the right choice.*

Rosa and Carla must have begun preparing the dinner early in the morning as the long table was filled with a complete Mexican home-cooked food featuring the authentic Mexican grilled goat.

Dallas was surrounded on each side by two beautiful women, Lori and Carla both sitting close to him, both adding food to his already full plate and refilling his wine glass. He smiled and tried not to pay more attention to Carla then Lori, as Lori was the primary woman in his life, and Carla was a good friend, and he hoped to keep it that way.

Romon smiled at Dallas and raised his wine glass in front of him. "To our dear friend from Texas. May you always grace our home, and we pray for you a long and prosperous life."

Rosa said in her sweet voice, "Salud, may you continue to live all the days of your life."

"I have a toast to make," Christian said as he stood up from his chair. "To my good friend and adopted big brother, Dallas McCall. I love you."

Dallas attempted to hide the tears welling up in his eyes. "I love you also, little brother. I thank you for permitting me to come into your home and the friendship that has grown into love for each other. Carlos will always be with us in spirit."

Lori placed her hand on Dallas's leg and looked at him in admiration. *Lord, I love this man. I only hope that he loves me as I love him.*

It was near five-thirty when Dallas and Lori bid goodbye to the Garcia family as they drove down the lane to the main road that would take them back to Lori's house.

Lori said, "That was wonderful, I really enjoyed being with the family. They are so respectful of you, and I got the feeling that you are part of their family."

Dallas nodded his head. "Yes, I think so, and I am honoured that they look at me as part of their family. I only wish Carlos was with us to enjoy the good life Diego and Badger took away from him. I will never forgive them that's for damn sure. "

"What are your plans now that your mission is complete?" Lori asked.

"I've been giving thought to going back to my home in Texas. My parents have a large cattle ranch, and they are not getting any younger. You ever been to Texas?"

"No, I have not. Just the sound of Texas intrigues me. I would love to wake up to green grass and morning doves singing outside my bedroom window."

Dallas said slowly, "Would you like to come with me for a visit to my home?"

She flung her arms around his neck and squealed, "I would love to go with you. Do you think that your family would like me?"

Dallas laughed. "What is there not to like about you. When can you be ready to travel?"

"Soon. Jose will take care of the garage with no problems while the new buyers are working on the finances to buy the garage. The sell on my house will be final next week. Say, the day after tomorrow, I can be ready to travel."

"Good. I'll take care of the transportation. It makes me happy that I can show off your beauty to my family and friends."

Dallas stopped by the house of his old Mexican woman friend, Francisca Alvarez, to thank her for her help and tell her goodbye. "We never got around to drink that beer," Dallas told her.

She laughed. "Next time when you are in town, we will have that beer and lunch. Oh, you can bring that pretty lady, Lori Porter, along with you."

Dallas laughed. "News travels fast around this small town."

He made one last trip in the Jeep, cruising around the streets that were once virtually empty when he arrived at seeing people walking in and out of stores and gathered in small mixed groups of Anglos and Hispanics talking, laughing having a good time among friends.

Epilogue

Monday morning, November 26, 2018, Dallas is silent as he walked onto the AMTRAK train platform, Lori smiling walking by his side.

He paused looking at the Garcia family standing in front of the townspeople who shunned him since the day he arrived on the train from Texas. He smiled at Carla, Romon, Rosa, and Christian, and Lori waved to them and blew a kiss. Carla stepped forward and pointed to Dallas and moved her mouth without speaking, *"I love you."* He nodded and thought that he saw moisture in her eyes.

Lori saw the interaction between Dallas and Carla. She smiled and hooked her arm through his. *He's mine*, she said to herself.

The gray-haired conductor welcomed them with a smile as they boarded. "Nice to see you again, Mr McCall. Are you going back to Texas?"

"Yes, sir. Happy to see your smiling face again."

The conductor stepped closer to Dallas and handed him a white envelope. "A man at the train station in Dallas asked me to deliver this to you. I saw him get into the back door of a black SUV. The car sped away followed by another black SUV."

Dallas glanced at the envelope with his name printed on the front. He placed it in his jacket pocket, smiled and nodded at the conductor.

As the train pulled away from the station, Dallas saw Sheriff Dan Baker standing in front of his SUV patrol vehicle. Further down the tracks. Mrs Norris, the owner of the Little Creek Bed and Breakfast waving at the train not knowing where Dallas and Lori were sitting.

Dallas stored the luggage and sat down next to Lori who sat in a window seat smiling.

The train gathered speed, heading down the rails toward Big Spring, Texas. Dallas smiled as he saw Lori's happy face looking out of the window of the train at the New Mexico landscape passing before her.

Somewhere out there in the foothills lay Diablo Ridge, waiting for the sun to crest over the spirit of my friend, Carlos. Take care, my brother. He wiped a tear from his eye and placed his hand on the hand of the beautiful woman sitting beside him smiling, the morning sunlight streaking through her red hair.

Dallas removed the envelope from his jacket pocket, ripped it open and unfolded the bond paper. "Mr McCall. We would like to speak to you about your future. Please call me on this private number. 505-825-4800. Regards, James R. Carter, Director, CIA Covert Affairs."

Now, that sounds interesting. I might just give Mr Carter a call!

Printed in the USA
CPSIA information can be obtained
at www.ICGtesting.com
LVHW022234020224
770781LV00002B/245